PIPED CROAKIES

SAM CHEEVER

ELECTRIC PROSE PUBLICATIONS

The Pied Piper shall lead them all astray...A captured audience helpless to its sway. The pipe's infectious music bids them come...and come they will...two by two or one by one.

Just when I thought my life couldn't get any weirder, life upped the strangeness quota to a never-before-seen level.

When a long line of critters, dazed and seemingly oblivious, marched past Croakies, I knew we had a *situation* on our hands.

Actually...if you counted being unwillingly affianced to a big old pink ogre...I had more than one situation.

Le sigh.

Then someone died. A king declared war on Enchanted. And my situation became a *crisis*. It would be up to me to find the perpetrator and bring him to justice while wrangling the rogue pipe artifact he used for his nefarious deeds.

Buffalo buttocks! I really do need a vacation.

STAY IN TOUCH

Sam doesn't give away a lot of books. But she values her readers and, to show it, she's gifting you a copy of a fun book just for signing up for her newsletter!

SIGN UP FOR SAM'S NEWSLETTER!

https://samcheever.com/newsletter/

1

PRESTIDIGITATION, LEGALESE, AND LARCENY

"We need an anti-ogre ward on the front door," Sebille growled before flinging two garment bags onto Shakespeare's desk, where I was studying ogre law.

I frowned at the bags. "What are these?"

Rather than respond, she reached over and unzipped the one on top, pulling it open to show me something from a fashion nightmare.

I shook my head, widening my eyes at her. "A really ugly dress? Where did it come from?"

"Where do you think, Naida!" she screamed, surprising even herself if the excessive blinking was any indication. She scrubbed a hand over her face, her hand shaking. "Sorry. This stupid wedding thing has me twisted in knots."

I could certainly understand that. I was spending ten hours a day, to the detriment of all my other work, trying to find a loophole in the contract we'd signed.

"These are supposed to be our wedding dresses." She grimaced. "I'm not marrying that ogre," she told me, her tone seeming to imply that I thought she should.

I raised my hands in self-defense. "I'm with you. We're not going to marry them. Even if we need to take a really long vacation on another dimension to avoid it."

She nodded, appearing mollified.

I tugged the bag away from the fluffy pink, black, and white dress, grimacing at the abundance of tule puffing out through the middle and over the hips. The dress seemed custom-made for ensuring its wearer looked thirty pounds heavier than she was. I forced my lips to uncurl and held it in front of Sebille. "At least you have the figure to make the most of this," I told her, earning a sour look in response.

"That's *your* dress, Naida."

I was pretty sure all the color drained from my face. "What? No. It can't be."

She showed me the card that had been shoved into a small pocket near the hanger. My name was scrawled over the cream-colored square in heavy black ink.

Whatever blood I had left in my face fled south. My five-foot-eight-inch, slightly fluffy frame would look terrible in the dress. "I can't wear this! I'll look like a really big piece of ugli fruit."

Sebille snorted. "You will. Thank goodness mine is more tasteful."

I cast a jaundiced blue eye over her current outfit of a short-sleeved forest green dress with hot pink polka dots, which she wore over striped pink and purple socks that disappeared beneath the flounce which landed below her knees and were tucked into her usual shiny red Wicked Witch of the West shoes. At least the shoes matched her fire-engine-red hair.

As usual, her fashion choices literally hurt the eyes and were an assault on good taste. "You don't say?" I responded.

Sebille rolled her eyes. "You're just jealous."

I flapped my lips, not sure what direction to go, and then gave up, shoving the nightmare in tulle toward the bag. "If I wasn't already determined to avoid this wedding, that dress would be enough to do it."

Sebille flopped down into Casanova's chair, twitched unhappily as the over-sexed furniture pinched her left buttock, and then reached down to smack the velvet seat hard enough to make the chair jump and try to scurry away. The sprite flung an immobility spell at the unfortunate thing, and it screeched to a halt on the concrete. Finally, the horrid piece of perverted furniture had met its match.

The door dividing the bookstore from the arti-fact library opened, and a tiny face peeked through. "Miss?" Hobs, our resident hobgoblin, said. "Something's wrong."

I closed my eyes, striving for calm. Something was always wrong. Casanova's chair creaked as Sebille stood up. "I'll go," she said crankily. "You keep looking for that loophole."

Sighing, I shoved the garment bags aside and bent over my book again. *Prestidigitation, Legalese, and Larceny in Ogrish Law: How to Maneuver around the Rocklike Obstinance of an Ogre King's Law* wasn't exactly compelling reading. Nor was it particularly helpful. My uncle Archibald Pudsnecker, a.k.a. Pudsy, told me the hard-to-read tome was my best chance to find a way out of the contract Sebille and I had signed without reading the small print.

In our defense...and I believed it was a really good defense...the contract had been written on the wide, pudgy back of the ogre king. It was a long contract, and the part that got us into trouble was located in the nether regions. And I mean that literally.

I'd closed my eyes and slashed the pen over my side of the posterior parchment without studying the last paragraph of the diabolical contract.

I'd know better next time. Fool me once; shame on you. Fool me twice, and I'd put holes in your posterior paper with a quill pen.

The door opened again. Sebille's head poked through. "Um, Naida."

I dropped my forehead onto the book, pounding it a few times against the aged pages. My long, brown hair flew around my head from the repeated blows.

She ignored my tantrum. "You're going to want to see this."

I lay there another beat and then sat up with a sigh. "I'm coming."

When I came through the door, I frowned at the sight in front of me. Mr. Wicked, Fenwald, Mr. Slimy, Hobs, and our newest member of the Croakies household, Baca the brownie, were all lined up along the windowsill, staring at something on the street.

What was really strange wasn't so much that they were lined up there. It was the way they all sat, so completely still, that seemed unnatural enough to give me pause.

Especially Hobs. He rarely sat still at all, let alone for any length of time.

I glanced at Sebille. "What's wrong with them?"

"Huh?" She frowned at me. "Not them, Naida." She motioned for me to follow her to the window.

Not a single one of my housemates looked up when Sebille and I joined them. I looked out at the scene in the street and felt my eyes go wide. "That's..."

I fell into a kind of daze, watching the parade on the street with uncommon focus.

A long line of animals, lined up as far as I could see in both directions, moved quickly past without so much as a glance from side to side.

Cats walked in front of dogs. Dogs walked in front of ferrets. Ferrets walked in front of bunnies. Bunnies hopped in front of squirrels. Birds flew above frogs, and frogs hopped in front of ducks.

It took me a moment to yank myself out of the light trance the sight had dropped me into. I literally shook it off and stepped away from the window, feeling dread tightening my chest. "What's that about?"

No response. I glanced at Sebille and discovered that she was enthralled as I'd been. "Sebille?"

Silence.

I reached over and poked her shoulder with a finger. She blinked and frowned. "Ouch, Naida."

"You were in a trance."

She rolled her eyes. "Of course I wasn't."

I shook my head. She had been. "Do you have any idea what's going on out there?"

"Not a clue. I tried to go outside, but the door wouldn't open."

"What do you mean, the door wouldn't open?"

"I mean, it wouldn't open. It was like there was some kind of spell holding it closed."

I hurried over to the door and turned the knob,

pulling it open. Giving my assistant a look, I arched a brow.

"I'm not lying, Naida," she snapped. "It wouldn't open before."

I stepped outside and looked around. The street was empty. "Where'd they all go?"

"Naida?"

I turned at the familiar voice of my friend Leandra. Lea was an earth witch, and she had an herbal shop next to Croakies. She was standing on the sidewalk outside *Herbal Remedies with Mystical Properties*, looking slightly dazed. Mr. Wicked's littermate, Hex, was clutched tightly in her arms. "Did you see that?"

I frowned down the street. "They were just here. Did you see where they went?"

Lea looked more spooked than I'd ever seen her. And that was saying something because she and I had been in some really weird situations together. "I was tugging on the door, trying to get out here. I couldn't open it. And then it suddenly..." She stared at her hand, her voice trailing off.

Sebille hit the sidewalk, all three cats and Slimy in her wake.

I threw a panicked look at the shop, but she shook her head. "I told Hobs and Baca they needed to stay out of sight."

"Good." The last thing we needed was for the humans in the neighborhood to see a hobgoblin and a brownie standing on the street.

Lea walked over and placed Hex on the sidewalk next to the other cats. The three of them immediately started twining together like some kind of furry, three-looped infinity symbol.

Something bad is coming, Slimy said inside my head. I nodded, knowing he was right. Residual energy bit along my arms, and a sulfurous stench still clung to the air. I looked at Sebille. "Talk to your mom. Maybe she can read the energy signature and tell us what that was."

For once, Sebille didn't argue. She strode away toward the enormous greenhouse behind Lea's shop. Her mother, Queen Sindra of the Enchanted fae, was currently living in the huge space, paying Lea for her hospitality by making her garden grow. The queen had recently been making noises about moving to one of the magical forests nearby. But, so far, she hadn't made any serious movement in that direction. Lea...and even though she'd never admitted it, Sebille...were hoping she didn't. I had to agree. The queen was powerful. But more importantly, she was experienced in the ways of the magical community. She'd been a vital ally for us on many occasions.

"Did you hear the music?" Lea asked.

Ripped from my thoughts, I turned a blank look in her direction. "Huh?"

"The music? It wasn't like anything I'd ever heard. It was strangely..." She frowned. "I'm not sure how to describe it." She placed a hand over her belly. "It felt like fingers grabbing my guts and tugging me forward."

I hadn't felt that. Had I? "I didn't hear any music," I told her, hoping I wasn't lying. I had a vague feeling that I might have heard something, but I didn't think it was music.

"It didn't sound like music," said a voice from the street.

Lea and I looked up to find our friend Rustin striding toward us. Sadie, his tiny amalgamate dragon, was perched on his shoulder, her rainbow-hued wings lifting and falling with every step. The usually cheerful little dragon appeared subdued.

Rustin was a little older than me, in his late twenties, with a strong jaw, a piercing blue gaze, thick black hair, and the cutest pair of wire-rimmed spectacles sitting on his classically perfect nose.

"Hey," I greeted my friend.

He stepped onto the sidewalk, and Sadie flew off his shoulder as he stopped. She joined the cats and the frog on the sidewalk behind us. "It was more like a hollow chiming sound," Rustin said. He frowned, rubbing his temple almost absently with two fingers. "It gave me the devil of a headache."

Sadie rose off the concrete, giving him a little trill as she fluttered around us with almost manic excitement.

He nodded. "Sadie says it was a lullaby. Like her mother used to sing to her."

I looked at Lea, lifting a brow in question.

Still rubbing her stomach as if it pained her, the witch seemed to be considering her response to my unspoken question. "I'm not sure. I have a vague impression of a specific memory. I was sitting around a campfire at Enchanted Lake with a bunch of my friends. Somebody was singing. It was a beautiful, haunting melody. That's what I heard."

"Odd," Rustin said. He shoved his glasses up his nose. His piercing blue gaze was contemplative. "It's definitely some kind of magic."

"But focused on animals?" I asked, shaking my head. "I've never seen anything like that before."

"It's a spell of some kind," Lea said. "I'd stake my store on it."

Judging by the sulfurous stench it had left behind, I tended to agree. I settled a speculative gaze on the small group of our animals, which had grown bored and were heading back into the store to see what trouble they could get into. "We need to find out what that was. If it was an artifact, I need to wrangle it. The potential for it being used for bad things is monumental."

"I agree," Rustin and Lea said in unison.

Lea nodded toward the disappearing backside of my mentor's black cat. "What's Fenny doing here?"

I sighed. "Alice showed up with him last night.

Apparently, she's going to be island hopping for the next month. She's in search of a magical pitcher of Margaritas." I peaked my brows as Lea laughed.

"Margaritas, huh?" Rustin said, grinning. "The cat doesn't like Margaritas?"

"Fenwald tends to chunder when Alice moves around too much. At least that's what she keeps insisting." I shrugged. "I don't mind. I've actually come really close to telling her to just leave him here. Being around the other cats is good for him. And he's good company."

"That's a great idea," Lea said. "She can come for visits whenever she misses him."

I grimaced. "Way to talk me out of it," I told her.

"I'm going to go research music-based spells," my friend told me. "I'll let you know what I find out."

"Thanks," I told her. "We're getting Sindra's opinion too. And I'll research possible artifacts."

I turned to Rustin as Lea headed back into her shop. He was staring off down the street, tension evident in the way he was holding himself. "What?" I asked my friend.

He gave a little twitch and turned to me. "Huh?"

"What's got you so bothered?"

"I have a really bad feeling about this, Naida."

I couldn't agree more. "Slimy thinks it portends bad things."

"I agree." He pointed toward Croakies. "Do you mind if Sadie has a play date today? I'm going to do some research too. Between all of us, we should be able to figure this out."

"It's fine. I'm sure they're all in the artifact library by now. Wicked is probably leading them on a dust bunny adventure."

Rustin's smile was tight. "Great. I'll let you know what I figure out."

2

DON'T YOU WANT TO GET BUGGY AND HELP?

A soft whirring sound was the only warning I got that Queen Sindra had arrived. Sebille came around the corner a moment later, her expression concerned.

"Hello, Naida," said the queen. Her familiar voice, so unlike her daughter's, was melodic and kind. The volume of her speech was normal, as if she weren't the size of a large dragonfly. "It's nice to see you again."

I fought a smile. The fae queen was always so polite...almost formal in her speech. She never missed a chance to be gracious.

Again...so unlike her daughter.

Sindra buzzed along the street, her colorful wings a blur on the air. Any humans who might be looking would only see a bug buzzing around. Perfectly harmless.

Sebille stood beside me, wringing her hands. I glanced at her, frowning at her unaccustomed jumpiness. "What?" I asked.

She gave her head a quick shake, watching her mother like a hawk.

"Don't you want to get buggy and help?" I asked my assistant. It wasn't like her to stand on the sidelines.

Sebille's frown deepened.

I opened my mouth to browbeat her into telling me what was wrong, but Sindra chose that moment to buzz back our way. "Inside," the queen said, shooting through the open door into Croakies.

We followed her in, knowing she was right. The harmlessly buzzing bug would take on a different feel altogether if the neighbors saw us standing on the street talking to it.

I closed the door and flipped the sign to Closed. The last thing I needed was for one of my human customers to pop in while we were chatting it up with the queen of the Enchanted fae.

The queen settled onto the small table near the bookshelves. She started to pace as soon as her tiny feet hit the surface, her hands twining in front of her.

Sebille and I shared a look. The queen was noticeably upset. That didn't bode well for whatever was happening in Enchanted.

"What is it?" I asked. "Are we dealing with a monster? Or an artifact?"

Her expression tightened. "I'm afraid it's both."

I sank onto a chair. "Great."

"I'm assuming this is the handiwork of the Pied Piper?" Sebille asked her mother.

Sindra nodded. "Unfortunately, yes."

I frowned as a memory danced through my mind, unable to capture it.

Fenwick sauntered through the dividing door, his raggedy ears twitching as he spotted the bug-sized queen. Looking at him, I finally caught the memory I'd been trying to grasp. It was something I'd learned when training to become Keeper under Alice, Fenwald's owner. "I thought the Piper had lost his pipe a few centuries ago. If I remember right, a Keeper of the Artifacts locked it into a vault."

Sindra nodded. "He'd compelled an entire population of a country town in the Shire to walk off a cliff." She paled at the thought. "Evil business. The PTB sentenced him to a millennia in the Hell dimension and declared that he would never be reunited with his pipe. But, before they could carry out the sentence, he disappeared."

The Powers that Be were one level of the magical hierarchy that ensured magic and magic users didn't step outside accepted bounds and harm either the magical or human worlds.

At the top of the hierarchy was a Universal

Council that ruled from an undetermined interdimensional space, where they kept watch on all of the dimensional representatives. Keepers of the Artifacts, or KoAs like me, were near the bottom of the pecking order. Each dimensional space had its own KoA and only one. Keepers answered to the Powers that Be, which, in turn, answered to the Council. Like Keepers, there was only one PTB per dimensional space. Outside of extraordinary circumstances, they weren't allowed to cross into another PTB's dimension or interfere with their activities.

I wasn't exactly sure how the Société of Dire Magic fit into the hierarchy. They seemed to be mostly an educational organization. Though they did perform trials for magic users and managed the prison system for supernormals on the earthly dimension.

"If his pipe was taken away from him, how could he be using it now?" I asked.

Sindra shook her head, her long, auburn hair glossy in the overhead light. "I have no idea. But I promise I'll do everything I can to find out."

After Sindra left, Sebille murmured something about doing some research and disappeared into the artifact library. I glanced at the frog clock on the wall and saw that it was time to close the book store. Leaving the Closed sign in the window, I followed her out of the bookstore. My stomach rumbled and I realized it was close to dinner time.

I knew I should eat but didn't feel like fixing anything. I was worried. Sindra's announcement had painted ice along my spine and made it hard to breathe. If the Piper from my studies was back, Enchanted was in grave danger.

My cell rang and I looked at the ID. It was Detective Wise Grym. Aka, my boyfriend, the cop, who also happened to be a gargoyle. "Hey," I said as I answered. "I don't suppose you feel like bringing tacos over?"

"I'm afraid the tacos will have to wait. We have a crisis."

"What crisis?"

"It's the ogres."

I bristled, feeling the unspoken pressure in his words. "Sebille and I are taking care of it. We could really use some support from you, by the way. Bursting into laughter every time we mention our ill-fated engagements isn't exactly helpful."

"Not *that* crisis, Naida. This is a real crisis."

Funny, I thought being forced to marry someone *was* a real crisis. "Has something happened to the king?"

King Rhorr ruled the ogres. He'd been the one at the center of tricking Sebille and me to become engaged to his people. He was a crafty old dude who sat naked on his throne when people came to call.

A very disconcerting habit, let me tell you.

But there was something about him. Looking into his sparkling gaze, so filled with good humor and fun, I couldn't bring myself to dislike the guy.

Also, he'd helped us out once when we'd had to pass through his kingdom to fight a battle with a crazy cupid.

Long story.

"Rhorr's fine," Grym told me. "But something's wrong there. He all but demanded that I come."

My eyes went wide. "What happened?"

"To tell you the truth, I don't know. Rhorr was really upset. He said something about an artifact, so I thought it probably made sense for you to come with me. Are you available?"

"Of course. And we can get tacos on the way home...right?"

He chuckled softly. "Would I be able to stop you?"

"Not a chance. I'm starving."

"I'll pick you up in ten minutes."

I knew Grym was the right man for me the moment I slid into the seat. He held a greasy bag that smelled like heaven in my direction. "I figured you'd need your strength for this."

I kissed him on a warm, bristly cheek and grabbed the bag with Taco Loco's logo on it. Clutching it to my chest, I inhaled the delightful fragrance. I gave Grym cow eyes. "Marry me?"

He laughed, pulling away from the curb. "Sorry, you're already spoken for."

I glowered over the bag at him. "Har."

He caught me eyeing the contents of the bag, my lower lip caught between my teeth. "Go ahead. I don't expect you to wait."

"Are you sure? I don't want to be rude."

His smile was slightly guilty. "I might have already eaten mine on the way to your place."

"Hey!"

He shrugged. "It's been a busy day. I haven't eaten since breakfast."

I happily dug in, consuming my three tacos by the time Grym pulled into the gravel parking lot at the edge of Rhorr's kingdom. Cars weren't allowed inside the boundaries. Not because of any environmental impulse, but because the entire thing was strewn with boulders and constructed of mountains upon ridges upon elevations.

The ogres were a rock-loving people, and a lot of

the formations within the kingdom were actually the faces of portals. We'd used one of those portals in the previously mentioned battle against the homicidal love deity.

As we picked our way across the difficult, uneven terrain, I was happy Grym had given me food before we came. I wouldn't have had the stamina to make it otherwise.

I kept expecting our betrothed, Rick and Maxine, to pop out at us as they had that fateful day...when we'd signed an ogre's contract without reading the fine print.

Big mistake.

But Rick and Maxine didn't pop out, and their absence somehow made our being there seem more ominous. "What exactly did Rhorr say?" I asked Grym.

He threw me a look and then frowned. "He said something had happened, and he didn't understand it. The only way he could explain it was if it was an artifact."

Since the ogres had one of the largest, unofficial repositories of non-lethal magical artifacts in the earthly dimension, that concerned me. The only way he wouldn't be familiar was if they were dealing with something toxic.

"Was anybody hurt?" I couldn't help thinking about Rick and Maxine. I had no desire to marry one of them, but they were pleasant enough creatures. I didn't want to see them get hurt.

To my chagrin, Grym nodded. "Several of the ogres were apparently injured."

A small sound escaped my lips and Grym glanced my way, his expression contrite. "Sorry. I should have prepared you for that. You know how sturdy these guys are. It's likely that nothing short of a rocket would seriously dent them."

I nodded, my thoughts spinning. "So Rhorr has no idea what kind of artifact?"

"No. Let's just keep an open mind and a positive thought until he fills us in. Maybe Rhorr was overreacting." Grym nudged me with a broad shoulder and smiled. "You know they're all about the drama."

They certainly were. Sebille and I had stopped directly denying that we were going to marry the ogres. The last time I'd done it, Maxine had threatened to fling herself off the highest peak of Mount Enchanted.

I sighed. "I'll try. But I have a bad feeling about this."

Grym didn't respond.

We came around a large pile of massive boulders that formed a kind of mini-mountain and jolted to a stop at the scene before us.

Hundreds of ogres covered the space between rocky outgrowths, many of them battered and bloody. The one nearest us was lying flat on her back, a blocky green hand covering what looked like an enormous goose egg on her forehead. Her knees and elbows were covered in wounds, a couple of them deep and still bleeding.

Not far from her was a small group that I determined had to be a family, though the "children" were enormous, probably in their teens. They all had wounds similar to the female closest to us, though one of the smallest ogre's legs, probably a female judging by her size and hairstyle, was bent at an odd angle. She was sobbing wildly as someone tried to wrap the broken limb.

Some of them moved as though in a daze. A few had wide bandages encircling their blocky heads. A larger group of around twelve ogres surrounded a relatively small crumpled form with long, blue-gray hair and gnarled fingers. The female's eyes were closed, and her yellow skin had a grayish tint to it. Her knotty fingers clutched the hand of a large male who was crouched at her side, his lips moving over words I couldn't hear.

The air was filled with the sounds of moaning, sharply spoken commands, and crying.

"Goddess in a rockslide," I muttered as Grym gripped my arm, tugging me forward. He bent his head close to mine and spoke very softly. "Move slowly, don't make any noise. We need to make it to Rhorr without drawing any attention."

I nodded, remembering the big ogre Grym and

fellow cop and wolf shifter Devin Sampson had battled on a previous visit. Even in their shifted forms of gargoyle and wolf, the two powerful men had barely held their own against a single ogre.

We were looking at hundreds of them. More ogres, in fact, than anybody had ever seen together in one spot. They tended to blend into their surroundings, observing and acting only if they sensed their land or people were in danger. In their current injured and stunned state, they'd most likely attack first and ask questions of our pulpy corpses later.

"Naida!" My gaze jerked up, and I spotted a giant pink form a dozen yards away, in the shade caused by the enormous pile of rocks.

"Maxine," I told Grym, and then, my heart pounding painfully in my chest, I took off running toward her.

3

THAT DOESN'T GET ANY EASIER WITH REPETITION

The female ogre was draped over a rock, her massive pink-skinned form bloodied and bruised. She had tears in her purple eyes, and her matching boy shorts and tank top were dirty and torn. She shoved a curtain of golden hair off her round face, her oversized features tight with pain. Still, despite it all, she smiled when I approached, holding out a hand. "You came."

I took the hand, which made mine look like a toddler's resting on the enormous palm. "Are you okay?" I asked stupidly. Of course, she wasn't okay. She was badly hurt.

Her smile widened. "I'm fine. Just resting a bit. The healer will be here as soon as she can."

I nodded, suddenly aware of a ruckus behind me. Maxine and I both turned our heads, and my gaze widened in alarm at the sight.

Grym, who'd wisely shifted to his gargoyle form, was fighting off two enormous male ogres as best he could. Unfortunately, he was badly outgunned in the effort. As a gargoyle, Grym was big and bulky, his muscles the density and hardness of actual rock. But he looked small between the two ogres. He was already sporting several gashes, and he was limping.

With a jolt of clarity, I realized the battle was my fault. The ogres were discombobulated and likely feeling defensive and enraged by whatever had happened to them. Grym had told me to move slowly and quietly. I'd ignored his sage advice, and He was paying the price for that. "No!" I yelled, standing straight. I pulled my keeper magic into my hands and prepared to fling it at them, even knowing it would do little to improve Grym's chances. I just didn't have that kind of defensive firepower.

As a dinner-plate-sized fist connected with Grym's blocky jaw and sent him flying through the air, I changed my mind and threw out my magic to call any available artifacts to me.

The magic didn't have time to work before a growl emanated from behind me. "Stop!" Maxine bellowed at the two ogres. What followed was a string of indecipherable words, shouted in the ogre female's high-pitched voice. Though I had no idea what Maxine was saying, the words had an effect on the two ogres beating up Grym.

They stopped, turned to Maxine, and growled out some kind of response.

I used the opportunity to slip past them and hurry over to Grym. *Holy slug snot!* "Are you okay?" It seemed like I was asking that a lot.

Grym sat up with my help, groaning softly. "That doesn't get any easier with repetition."

I grinned. "Maybe you should reconsider doing hand-to-hand battle with ogres."

He served me up a wry look, the effect emphasized by his rock-like features. "Why didn't I think of that?"

"Sorry," I told him. "That was my fault." I helped him get to his feet, but he didn't change back to his human form. I couldn't really blame him for that.

Maxine came over to us, limping slightly. She placed a hand on Grym's shoulder and patted him hard enough to drive him into the ground like a fence post. "Good battle, Wise Grym. You're a strong male. I have just the female for you."

Grym gave a panicked chuckle, holding up his hands. "No, thanks. I'm good."

Maxine's golden brows lifted. "Would you prefer a male?"

Grym's answering chuckle sounded slightly choked. "No. But thanks."

She nodded, wrapping an enormous arm around my shoulders. "Fiancé Naida. I should have asked.

Did you come for a visit?" She frowned. "I don't have gifts or flowers."

She looked so distraught I felt guilty. Which was ridiculous. "No. We came because the king called us. He said something happened with a rogue artifact?"

Maxine frowned toward the distant horizon. The land stretched brown and lumpy with rocks and elevations as far as the eye could see. In the distance, the Enchanted Mountain range pierced a low-lying bank of fluffy white clouds. It formed an arresting, if not quite beautiful picture. "Whatever did this to us, it was definitely rogue. I'm not sure the artifact was to blame," she said.

Okay, that wasn't unsettling. No, not at all. "What do you mean?"

"A figure came through our land." She frowned. "A strange creature."

"Strange how?" Grym asked.

"He was unformed," said a deep voice behind us. We turned to find King Rhorr coming toward us, thankfully wearing a robe similar to the one he'd worn the last time I was there. The sun transformed the red of the velvet robe into a ruby-like hue and sparkled in the fluffy white fringe that matched his wild mop of hair and flowing beard.

The king fixed bright blue, bead-like eyes on me, sans their usual twinkle. In fact, his entire demeanor was different from the times I'd met him before. He usually gave off a Santa Claus-type vibe that was reinforced by his twinkling eyes, rosy cheeks, and long, white beard. But the figure heading our way carried nothing of his usual bright charm "This creature came upon my lands uninvited and drew my people under a spell that caused hundreds great harm." He fixed the hard blue beads of his gaze on me. "I want him found. Then you shall give him over to me, and we will administer ogre justice."

I didn't know the exact shape of ogre justice. But I was pretty sure it wouldn't be pleasant.

Grym stepped forward, pulling the king's hard gaze from me. "Respectfully, King Rhorr, we need to go through the normal, legal channels on this. I understand that you're upset..."

"Upset!" Rhorr...well...roared. "He attacked my people! I want him torn limb from limb and spread on the rocks for carrion birds to peck apart. I want to walk past his corpse and spit on it until every last piece is gone. I want the story of his death to spread far and wide, instilling terror into the hearts of any and all who might consider doing what he did. This must never happen again."

Holy vulture vittles! "We'll find him, King Rhorr," I said in my calmest voice. "Whatever you can tell us about what happened will help."

The king's gaze slid away. He suddenly couldn't look me in the eye.

Grym and I waited.

After a moment, Rhorr sighed. "As I said, he was

unformed. Like a shadow moving across the land. And when I questioned my people, every single one said something different. One said she heard her favorite lullaby from when she was a child. Another claimed he heard the sound of trains in the distance. Another claimed she heard a hive of bees buzzing nearby." He frowned, his eyes narrowing above his bulbous nose. "Whatever the creature was, he had them in his thrall."

"Thrall?" Grym asked. "What did he make them do?"

Rhorr's dark eyes looked haunted. "They followed him like puppies enticed by mother's milk," he said, shifting on his big feet. His gaze found mine, and some of the rage leeched away to make room for fear. "They walked right off that ridge up there. And every last one of them had a smile on his or her face as they went over the edge."

"I need to make sure that Pied Piper artifact is still locked up," I told Grym.

He held the car door open for me and waited while I slid inside. It was something he'd started doing since we'd been kind of, sort of dating. It was nice.

"I'd like to know that too," he said, frowning.

"Although, if it's not, we have an even bigger problem than we know."

"What do you mean?" I asked.

Grym closed the door and came around the car, sliding behind the wheel. "Everything we've learned so far seems to point to us having a Pied Piper attack going on in Enchanted. But if the Piper's pipe artifact is locked up..."

"It means we're dealing with something totally different," I finished for him. "Something unknown."

"Yeah." Grym drove out of the gravel lot and headed back toward Enchanted. "At least if it's the Pied Piper, we can do some research and learn how to deal with him."

We drove in silence for a few minutes while I thought about the situation. What we'd all seen on the street in Enchanted had been weird and unsettling. What Rhorr just described was terrifying. And a pretty big escalation. "What do you think the objective is here?" I asked Grym.

"Objective?"

"Yeah. This piper, whoever it is, has to have a goal in mind, right?"

"Not necessarily. If I've learned anything over the years as a cop, it's that criminals sometimes just do stuff for fun. Even the sickest and most evil stuff." He turned onto Arcane Avenue and headed toward Croakies. "Also for power," he added after a moment's thought. "That's a big one. Bad people like to control others' behavior. We see it in the human world all the time. Their government is full of people like that."

"If that artifact is still in the Keeper's hands, we'll go to Plan B." Grym pulled up in front of Croakies and I climbed out of the car. "Call me later?" I asked.

"Count on it."

Croakies was quiet when I went inside. Mr. Slimy was in his terrarium near the tea counter, asleep on a flat rock underneath the heat lamp. I pulled the blanket over his glass house and glanced at the clock. It was nearly eight o'clock. The kids would have all put themselves to bed already, and Sebille was probably holed up in her miniaturized apartment.

The sprite had been kicked out of her old apartment across the street, the one Rustin was currently living in, for over-imbibing on her special blend of vape and turning the owner's favorite customer into a slug.

In her defense, she'd turned him right back. But his humiliation at the slime puddle he was left sitting in sent him into spasms of rage, which ultimately ended in Sebille being expelled.

So she'd moved into Croakies. With me. Yes, it was as horrible as you're probably thinking. Mostly because she snored. Loudly. And she filled my tiny apartment above the store with an abundance of furniture and...knickknacks. I would never understand why people kept knickknacks. Annoying things. Always wrapping themselves in dust.

Anyway...

After costing me several nights of sleep, Sebille suddenly stopped coming to my apartment above the shop. I eventually discovered that she'd made a home in a miniaturizing artifact. Basically a small metal box that shrunk any objects placed inside it. Which was good since Sebille had enough stuff for ten families. The nice thing about that kind of home was that, if you could fly like Sebille, you could stick it on a really tall shelf behind a bunch of other artifacts and nobody could find or bother you.

Which was why it had taken me months to discover where she'd moved.

I headed upstairs to do my thing, then sang the Muffin Man song to flush the magical toilet. I changed into my jammies, got myself a drink and a snack, and carried my goodies down to the library to settle myself at Shakespeare's desk.

My first task was to find out which KoA had charge of the Pied Piper's pipe. Thankfully, the desk came up with a user's manual of keepers and their assigned artifacts, making the task easier than you'd think given the number of dimensions and associated keepers.

The handy, dandy reference guide even included the artifacts alphabetically, magically updated as the inventory changed.

Perusing that book was more fun than watching two centipedes dance the tango.

As luck would have it, I found the pipe under Bandy Joe Barrows' name, which seemed appropriate given the current situation. Bandy Joe had established my bookstore, Croakies, before moving to his current dimension to open a shop of the same name. Joe had a deep love of frogs, to the point that he even kind of looked like one. But, despite his penchant for all things bug-eyed and hoppy, he was a nice guy and a great Keeper.

Plus, he already knew me, so there'd be no uncomfortable "getting to know each other" phase.

Ready for the next problem, I spun on my chair and sent an unhappy gaze toward my communication mirror. The artifact had recently been shattered during an unfortunate *enraged goddess* incident, and it was still in the process of repairing itself.

I needed that mirror to call on Bandy Joe. There were no interdimensional cell phones I could use. Or interdimensional data minutes. Other than using my communicating mirror, there was only one other way I knew of to contact someone on another plane.

I grimaced at the idea of inter-dimensional travel. It was a long, drawn-out affair of finding the right spot, climbing a lot of stairs, walking down an unending hallway, stepping into a painting, and then doing a terrifying freefall from a cloudy sky into a second Enchanted with a Croakies that looked just like mine.

That other Enchanted even had a Lea look-alike.

That was fun.

I sighed. "But is it worth it just to see Other Lea again?"

Something soft and warm brushed against my calf, and I jumped with a yelp. I hadn't expected to see Mr. Wicked downstairs again. He'd been curled up next to Fenwald in his usual spot on my bed when I'd gone up to put on my jammies. "Hey, buddy. What are you doing up?"

Ribbit!

I frowned at Mr. Slimy. "You too? What's going on?" I looked around, expecting more trouble to find me.

He's here because he came to get me, Slimy said. *Apparently, you need my help.*

I frowned down at the little green squish. He blinked bulgy black eyes at me. "What can you do to help?" I asked. I thought it was a reasonable question, but the frog puffed up with offense. *Believe it or not, I do have skills.*

The frog was right. He had skills. He saw magic in the air. He knew things. And sometimes he even seemed to foretell... I blinked. "Do you know something about this Pied Piper?"

What? No. Don't be daft.

My brows arched. "Daft?"

His squishy body rippled in what I assumed was a shrug.

"Then why are you here?"

I don't know, Naida. He snapped. *That's up to you to figure out. And if you don't mind, hurry up about it. It's cold in here, and I'm tired. I'm missing my favorite rock and my heating lamp.*

Wicked rubbed himself along the base of the standing communication mirror and meowed. I narrowed my gaze at him. What was he trying to tell me?

Bandy Joe Barrow's name passed through my head. "What I need help with is reaching out to Bandy Joe. I don't know how..."

It hit me hard, causing me to blink. Bandy's Joe's words drifted through my brain. *"I'm guessing then that you know what excellent magic conductors frogs are?"*

I hadn't known. And I'd since forgotten. "That's it!" I said, scooping up the frog.

Ahhh! He yelped unhappily. *Warn a guy first, would ya?*

"Sorry. I need to use this mirror, but it's not quite up to snuff. So, I'm hoping you can be a magic conductor for me?"

The frog's silence wasn't a good sign. I stared at him. "I said, I was hoping..."

I heard what you said, replied the cranky frog. *But*

it might as well have been gibberish. I have no idea how to be a conduit.

"The guy who originally named this store thinks you do," I told him. My cat meowed again. He was sitting at the feet of the cracked and chipped mirror, looking up at me. "Okay, buddy. I'll give it a try. Goddess knows you're usually miles ahead of me on this magic stuff. You probably know what you're talking about." I set the frog down on the floor in front of Wicked and straightened. Staring into the broken mirror, I took a deep breath and then said Bandy Joe's name.

I don't know what I was expecting, but it certainly wasn't a full-grown man suddenly stumbling out of the mirror, tripping over my feet, and slamming to the ground next to me.

Oops!

4

YOU DO LOOK PRETTY TASTY

Bandy Joe Barrows blinked up at me from his spot on the hard concrete. His bulgy black gaze looked a little dazed, and I hoped he hadn't hit his head when he'd landed.

"I'm so sorry," I said, crouching down to help him stand. "That worked a little better than I'd expected."

Bandy Joe was a little wobbly when I got him to his feet, so I pulled the chair from Shakespeare's desk over and urged him to sit.

"What happened?" he asked, still blinking rapidly.

Wringing my hands, I felt my cheeks flush with embarrassed guilt. "I was just trying to make a mirror call to you. But the mirror hasn't fully repaired itself yet. Then I remembered what you said about frogs being good magic conductors."

Bandy Joe skimmed his gaze to the frog sitting in front of the mirror. The two of them puffed their cheeks and blinked for a full minute as if in silent communication.

For all I knew, they could be doing a mind-meld. "That's Slimy," I said before I could stop myself. My cheeks flushed hotter as Joe skimmed me a disgusted glance. "Slimy?"

I winced. "Yeah. I wasn't much of a frog fan when I named him."

"You know frogs aren't slimy, right?" The indignant squaring of his rounded shoulders told me I'd mortally wounded him.

"I do. *Now* I do. I didn't then." A previous experience touching what I'd thought was a slime-covered "frog" that had given me hives had clearly left me with issues. I'd later learned that what I'd touched had most likely been a toad rather than a frog. Or else it had been cursed by a witch's spell to give hives.

Either way, in my simple brain, frogs meant bad. Frogs meant slime and hives. End of the fairytale.

Slightly mollified, Joe stood and bent to scoop up my frog. He petted him like a dog, grinning. "You are a powerful little guy, aren't you?"

"Ribbit!"

Joe giggled as if Mr. Slimy had said the cleverest thing he'd ever heard. The man was definitely a frog fan. He finally glanced at me. "So, Naida. What did you need help with?"

I grabbed the inventory book from the desk and showed it to him, pointing to the Pied Piper's pipe entry. "I needed you to confirm that this is still in your artifact library."

Joe stared at the entry for a beat and then nodded. "Of course. It's in my toxic artifact vault. Why do you ask?"

Turtle trousers! I sighed. "Because someone is enthralling people and animals in Enchanted with a Pied-Piper-like artifact. Today's attack was bad. Dozens of ogres were seriously hurt."

Joe's eyes went wide. "Ogres? Oh my. Is the king laying waste to the town?"

"No." My expression twisted with horror. "Why would he do that?"

Bandy Joe shrugged. "It's happened. Ogre kings can be rather volatile."

"He's definitely mad. Grym had to remind him justice wasn't his job."

"Speaking from experience, don't trust that the king will stand down. Ogres rarely recognize any authority over their own. They can be quite stubborn on the point."

Didn't I know it? Rhorr had resisted all the arguments we'd made against forcing Sebille and me to marry his people. It had been like talking to the fat squish in Bandy Joe's hands. A lot of blinking and very little changing of minds.

"I'll let Grym and the Société take care of that. I just need to isolate and wrangle that pipe. Any input you can give me would be greatly appreciated."

Bandy Joe inclined his head in agreement. "Do you have someplace where we can work?"

I indicated the desk, but he shook his head. "Somewhere we don't have to worry if the frog pees."

"Um..."

He patted my shoulder. "Do you have a table in the bookstore as I do?"

"I do, but..." *Ew!*

He jerked his head toward the dividing door. His Croakies being the same layout as mine, Joe knew his way around without my having to tell him. "I'll get us set up. You ask the desk for everything it has on the piper, including copycats."

Copycats? My brows went skyward. *Of course!* I sat down at the desk and got to work.

"I can't believe there isn't a single magical copycat to the Pied Piper," I groused two hours later. Joe and I sat in the middle of a dozen thick, leather-bound books that were open to spots where we'd hoped to discover clues as to what we were dealing with. I looked at him. "Is it possible we're dealing with the actual piper?"

Joe stretched his bowed legs out in front of him, groaning softly. "I suppose anything's possible."

"I was told he was sentenced to the Hell dimension but escaped before they could banish him."

Joe nodded. "Throughout history, there have been rumors...suspected pipers...none of whom were proven. Several serial killers have been compared to the piper," Bandy Joe said, warming to his topic. "But there have really been none who perfectly fit the piper's modus operandi. He seems to have simply disappeared."

"Has there been any speculation of his whereabouts?" I asked.

"Oh, my, yes. Tons. But it's just speculation." He seemed to consider it for a moment and then said. "There's a witch in my dimension who says she has proof the Piper is dead." He shook his head. "Nobody believes her because she claims he's a restless spirit who walks the Enchanted Woods at night, his pipe playing a cherished melody from times long past."

I thought about that. "She has proof?"

"That's what she says."

"I should probably talk to her."

"To what end?" Joe asked, frowning.

"If she knows where he was last seen, maybe we

can find him. It's possible he can tell us who's terror-izing us here and now."

"From what we know of the Piper, he's angry and distrustful. What makes you think he'll help?"

"I don't know that he will. But I feel like I have to at least try."

Joe shoved himself off the ground and offered me a hand. "Let's get this mess cleaned up and go talk to a witch."

I nodded. "We also need to figure out where *our* piper got a pipe like the one the real piper had."

"Excuse me?"

I shrugged. "You have the piper's magical pipe in your vault. That means the pipe being used here in Enchanted..."

"Has to be a copy." Joe scrubbed his hands over his face. "I'm an idiot. Somebody has to be making copies, and those copies are every bit as dangerous as the original."

"Yep. Which means we have several big problems instead of just one," I told him.

"Are you sure?" I asked the other KoA.

Bandy Joe shrugged. "It worked coming this way. Besides, setting up a visit to the portal will take time we don't want to waste. I have a feeling a visit to the witch is key to finding this fake piper."

I expelled air. Ever since the horrible experience of stepping into a magical black and white television artifact to rescue Hobs, Wicked, and Slimy, I've been really leery of giving myself over to magical objects.

Especially when my magical regulator was sitting on the floor, blinking blankly at me.

I narrowed my gaze on Slimy. "You sure you can handle this?"

I got him here, didn't I?

"Yeah," I responded, frowning. "But did you know what you were doing?"

Blink.

"That's what I thought."

Joe shook his head. "He's just the conduit, Naida. He doesn't need to know what we're doing. He just needs to...erm...conduit."

"Well, that certainly clears things up," I grumbled. I scooped up my cat.

Bandy Joe placed Slimy in front of the mirror, and we stepped back. He raised a hand, looking at me. "Ready?"

"No."

He grinned. "Where's your sense of adventure, girl?"

"It's hard to say. I could have left it in the evil town of Mayberry. Or maybe in the Jurassic era. I guess a wraith from the Enchanted Forest could have taken it when it tried to kill me..."

Bandy Joe sent energy into the mirror.

A heavy soft warmth smacked into my chest, and Wicked yowled as invisible hands grabbed me around the shoulders and yanked...

The world went inside out and shot sideways in a dizzying, out-of-control ride filled with flaring light and inconceivable darkness. I was vaguely aware of Bandy Joe next to me, but not as a living being. He was more like a collection of motes in the wildly fluctuating atmosphere. Inside my head, I was screaming like the banshee who lived across the street from Croakies.

I only hoped I didn't do permanent harm to anybody when we finally landed on the other side.

As if the thought had conjured our destination. I hit the ground hard enough to compact the bones in my legs and hips into two bumpy pancakes and rolled until I smacked up against something unyielding and rough.

I lay on a patch of smashed vegetation, inhaling a combo of fresh grass and fur. Everything in my body screamed with pain. "Ugh," I murmured.

"Yeow!" complained Wicked before jumping off my chest and sauntering away, tail snapping the air.

"Sorry, buddy." I wrenched my eyes open and looked up, up, up into the branches of an enormous tree. When I tried to sit up, bark sifted down on my face.

"Well, that was even less fun the second time," said Bandy Joe from a few feet away.

I turned my head to find him draped over a bush with dark green leaves and prickly-looking branches. "Are you okay?"

He grunted softly, shoving himself out of the bush. He sat in the grass and blinked at me. A beat later, he winced at something past my shoulder. "That must have hurt."

My gaze followed his line of sight, and I blanched at the unmistakable outline of someone my size and shape carved into the trunk of the enormous tree. The entire outline, complete with open, screaming mouth, was sans bark.

I looked down to find the aforementioned bark clinging to my clothes and, in a few cases, embedded in my skin. "Ah!"

As soon as I saw it, the wounds started to throb.

I jumped to my feet and started clawing at the offending chunks of wood.

Ignoring me, Bandy Joe glanced around at the overgrown woods, his bushy brows lowered in contemplation. "I believe the house is that way." He pointed a short, slightly bent finger into the woods at its most overgrown spot.

I eyed the direction he indicated. "Why is the story of Hansel and Gretel leaping to mind?"

He chuckled darkly. "It could be because it's apropos." He started walking.

"Wait, it's what?" I stumbled clumsily after him. "You're just joking, right?"

Joe smoothed a hand over a tree to the left of our "path" and sniffed his fingers before taking off again. "Not a joke. Endeara has been known to bake her enemies into pies and eat them."

I was pretty sure I didn't consciously jam my muscles into the lock position. But the result was the same whether I'd intended it or not. Suddenly, I couldn't take another step.

Joe turned back to me after a few steps, frowning. "Naida?"

I just shook my head.

He expelled a gust of frustrated air. "Do you want to save your people?"

I chewed my bottom lip.

He crossed stumpy arms over his broad chest and glared at me. "Really? You value your life over those of the people you care about?"

I chewed harder, my face taking on a permanent grimace. "She eats people," I said in what seemed to me a reasonable excuse for not just stumbling into her lair.

"Sometimes. But not often, Naida. Only when the moon is full and blue."

My gaze shot to the sky, and I winced at the big golden ball of the sun. We wouldn't know the state of the moon until it was too late to run. Why couldn't Bandy Joe's dimension run on the same time as mine? It was nice and dark at home.

"Naida?"

I gusted out a sigh. "All right. But I just want to go on record as greatly lamenting my current state of taco and eggroll flavored fluffiness."

He laughed. "You do look pretty tasty."

I trudged along beside him, pouting. "Story of my life."

5

OPTION 1, MAKE A RUN FOR IT

The Grimms brothers would have been right at home in the Enchanted Woods on Bandy Joe's dimension. It was a lot like the Enchanted Forest in my dimension, except that parts of it were clearly fed by darker magic. Death magic.

I could almost smell the rot of evil on the air as we moved deeper and deeper into the forest. The air was colder inside the woods. Frigid with evil intent. And if we weren't moving enough to take the edge off the cold, I'd have probably dropped into a fetal ball of ice a long way back.

As it was, my teeth were clacking together so hard I was worried I was going to fracture them before we finished our task and got out of there.

Even Wicked's endless feline confidence was being taxed by the suffocating sense of foreboding permeating the space. He'd started out scampering after bugs and leaping at falling leaves, but for the last mile or so, he'd stuck close to my legs, nearly tripping me from trying to press against my calves.

"Are we almost there?" I whispered to Bandy Joe.

He eyed me for a long moment, his breath coming out in little puffs of fog. "Why are you whispering?" he finally asked.

I shuddered violently, my teeth clacking ominously together. "I feel watchers all around us."

His gaze skimmed the arc of our surroundings, and he nodded. "Yep. They're everywhere."

I felt my eyes go wide as I followed the path of his gaze. Eye-shaped objects glowed yellow and red and even silver from the dense vegetation along the ground and shone through the rich umbrella of leaves overhead. The feral gazes were unblinking. They seemed to follow us as we moved forward along a path that was little more than a snail path through the greenery.

I bent close to Bandy Joe. "What are they?"

He shrugged, appearing unconcerned. But I saw the lines of strain around his bulging eyes and recognized the new tension in his bulky form. "They've been with us for over an hour. I figure if they were going to attack, they'd have done it by now."

I reached down and plucked Wicked off the ground, holding him tightly against my chest. It was proof of his unease that he didn't fight to escape my grip.

The dense blanket of trees suddenly broke apart in front of us, and I found myself staring at a tidy little house sitting in a neat little postage-stamp yard. Looking for all the world like an oversized gingerbread house sans candies, the little house was brown with white trim and had flower boxes filled with white roses beneath the two front windows. I'd never seen roses in a flowerbox. It was pretty. But it looked unnatural like the rest of the house.

Behind the glass of one window, orange-gold light flickered. Probably a fireplace.

I chewed my lip again, picturing an enormous fireplace that was large enough to cook a fluffy Keeper of the Artifacts.

"This is it," Bandy Joe said, his bulgy eyes riveted on the small house.

"We need a plan," I told him.

He nodded but didn't offer one.

After a moment of shared silence, I asked, "Do you have a plan?"

He turned a terrified gaze on me. "I thought maybe you could come up with one."

Panic flared in my breast. I pulled breath past the clog in my airpipes and released it slowly, trying to calm myself. "Okay. Option 1, make a run for it."

Despite his ashen complexion, Bandy Joe barked out a laugh. "Let's hold that one to the side for a bit."

I nodded. "Option 2…"

"Well, well, well," said a wobbly, razor-edged voice. "What have we here?"

I jerked so hard I bumped against Bandy Joe, nearly taking him off his feet. Thank heaven for his sturdy, bowed legs. They managed to keep us both upright as I spied the large, midnight-colored bird perched on a low branch.

"Meow!" threatened Wicked, his tail whipping the air in anticipation of a winged snack. What could I say? My cat thought he was a great panther. But his confidence was a sight to behold.

"Option 1?" I whispered hopefully.

Bandy Joe sighed, then stepped forward. "We've come to speak to Endeara."

I nodded jerkily, feeling like the cowardly lion in the Wizard of Odd.

The enormous, jet-black bird lifted its wings and glided smoothly toward the ground. It landed a few feet away and fixed a hostile black gaze on us.

I forced myself to breathe. It was the biggest raven I'd ever seen. I'd thought Madeline Quilleran's Rasputin was big, but this guy was at least twice his size.

Wicked tried to leap out of my arms, but I squeezed him tight. Overconfidence aside, the raven was big enough to carry Wicked away and do terrible things to him.

"What is your business with the witch?"

"We seek information."

I snuck a look at Joe, surprised he wasn't more forthcoming. If the witch didn't understand how important our visit was, she might refuse to see us. I opened my mouth just as the raven gave a little hop and then strutted like a rooster across the tidy grass of the yard. "How important is this information to you?"

The creature's sly tone had me snapping my mouth shut. Answering the question the wrong way would be dangerous. I thought about it for a minute and then said. "The information isn't important to us personally. But the potential for danger to the magical world is enough for us to have taken this journey. If Endeara doesn't care to hear our concerns, we'll just be on our way."

I started to turn away.

The raven lifted its wings and hopped toward me as if wanting to stop me from leaving.

Alarm twisted my heart into an erratic beat.

Wicked hissed, his claws digging into my arm in another escape attempt.

But the raven stopped, rippled its feathers, and then opened its beak, sending a beautiful melody into the air.

The music brought warmth to my icy limbs, and the heated ball of the sun suddenly rose above the trees, painting the ground in golden light.

Happy energy infused me. I smiled as memories

of my friends and the things I loved sifted through my mind.

I turned toward the little house. A golden aura bathed it, and the door stood open. A beautiful woman dressed in silver and gold, like an angel, beckoned me inside.

I took a step in that direction.

Agony scraped along the flesh of my arms, wrenching me out of the daydream.

"Ouch!" I yelled, glaring down at my cat and the bloody tracks he'd made with his claws. "What was that for?"

He twisted in my arms and finally gained freedom. Before I could snatch him back, he ran toward the house, which I noticed was no longer bathed in light. The door was no longer open.

I looked around, feeling dazed. "What just happened?" I asked.

Bandy Joe didn't answer me. He was doing the zombie shamble toward the house, a goofy smile on his face.

Oh. Okay.

I walked over and punched him in the stomach.

"Umph!" Joe bent double, wheezing.

I patted his back. "Sorry about that. The witch spelled us somehow."

He wheezed again. "You couldn't have just poked me on the shoulder?" Wheeze.

"Apparently, violence is the only thing that cuts

into this particular spell." I showed him my arm and he groaned, straightening slowly.

The door of the house opened, casting warm, golden light over the pristine white stepping stones leading to the front door.

I expected to see a warty old crone standing there. But the woman who stood in the doorway resembled the one in the spell, and I grabbed Bandy Joe's arm. "That's not good."

"Hello," the woman said in a kind voice. "Welcome to my home. Won't you come in for a snack?"

I jerked violently. "Snack? What did you have in mind?"

She frowned. "Cookies?"

My mouth watered. *Stupid, stupid Naida.* "You don't have a couple of children in your fireplace in there?"

She seemed surprised for a moment. Then she laughed. "Somebody's been reading too many fairytales."

I shrugged. "Just to clarify. If we come in there, do we have your word that you aren't going to eat us?"

The woman eyed me for a long moment...long enough to give me pause...then she burst out laughing, the sound not unlike the gorgeous melody the raven had sung. I tensed for the bespelled feeling to hit me again. It didn't come.

"Please, come inside. It's cold in the wood this time of night."

I blinked, looking around in shock to find out she was right. It was nighttime. When had that happened?

Mr. Wicked bounded over and rubbed against her legs, earning a bright giggle from the angelic-looking witch. "What a darling boy you are," she crooned. She looked at me, a sparkle in her eye. "Come, your familiar trusts me. You trust him, yes?"

I trusted him, yes. But I didn't trust the beautiful witch. Not even a little bit.

Bandy Joe started toward the house, and I reluctantly followed. Whatever the witch had up her sleeve, my cat was inside the house, and I couldn't leave him there.

She stepped back as I reached the door, her form wavering slightly before firming into something too beautiful to be real.

Was she real?

I watched her carefully as she glided around the room. She walked over and poked at an already blazing fire with a deadly-looking poker, and I couldn't help wondering if she was just stoking the fire to tweak me.

"Tea?" she asked with a bright smile. "Cookies?"

Joe and I declined. I stood as far from the fire as I could get and watched Wicked chase a cricket that had found its way inside the tidy little house.

"Please, sit. Tell me why you journeyed so far from your homes."

How did she know how far we'd journeyed?

"We have heard that you know something of the Pied Piper," Joe offered. He dropped lightly into an overstuffed chair before the fire, rubbing his hands together as he eyed the cricket.

His bulgy black gaze looked too much like a frog's, and my stomach roiled as I pictured him snatching the bug away from Wicked and stuffing it into his mouth.

I shuddered.

"Are you chilled?" asked the witch with a secret smile.

"I'm fine. What can you tell us about the piper?" I asked, forcing my mind on to equally unpleasant things.

"Why do you wish to know about him?"

Joe gasped and I turned to find him staring at me in horror. I blinked, my hand going self-consciously to my face. Did I have something disgusting there?

"Um..." I gave him a pointed look and turned my attention back to the witch. "We believe we have a copycat piper in my town. He's already attacked the ogres."

Endeara's eyes went wide, and she clapped glee-fully. "How fun!"

Okay, that wasn't exactly the reaction I'd been expecting. "The ogre king didn't think it was fun at all." My angry tone bounced off her like water off a duck-demon's back. "Pshaw! Rhorr likes to pretend affront. He's really much too emotional."

"You know him?" I asked, dread sliding icy fingers around my heart. The witch knew entirely too much about my world. "How is that possible?"

She flicked a hand. "I make it my business to know all the power players in nearby dimensions. It comes in handy."

I could imagine it would. "So, do you know of any copycat pipers?" I asked

She seemed to be considering my question. While I waited for her to respond, I watched Wicked pounce on the unfortunate cricket, munching it happily.

I grimaced.

A small gray mouse shot out from under the couch where the witch sat and scampered past me, stopping only the length of a single heartbeat to look up at me with its black bead eyes.

Bandy Joe made an outraged sound, and I looked over to find him glaring daggers at me.

I shook my head and turned my palms up in silent question.

His throat swelled and flattened, and his mouth opened. A long, sticky tongue snapped the air and came back laden with a fly.

"Oh!" I exclaimed, all the blood running from my face.

Joe looked at me like I'd lost my mind.

"...spirit for some time. I doubt he's your piper."

I forced my attention back to the witch. "Huh?"

She looked from me to Joe and frowned, then gave a girlish little laugh and flipped the fingers of her right hand in the air.

It was like someone had put a giant vacuum nozzle into the room and sucked all the air out, pulling fresh air in behind it.

I glanced at Joe, seeing him looking as surprised as I felt. But he appeared normal again. Less like a frog and more like the keeper I knew.

"As I was saying," said a raspy, slightly screechy voice.

I turned back to the witch and yelped, picking my feet up from the floor as if she were a mouse threatening to climb up my leg.

She grinned. The sight was terrifying.

6

SHOOTING LIKE A ROCKET ACROSS
THE ROOM

"Sorry about that," Endeara said. "I sometimes forget the effect my glamour has on others. Occasionally it creates subordinate delusions that wreak havoc with the mind."

I pressed back against the couch, my eyes ready to pop from my head. "Subordinate..." I breathed out, trying to understand what she meant.

Bandy Joe cleared his throat, his expression mostly neutral. Though I did notice a decided wobble in his chins, and his knuckles were white where he clutched the chair. "Well. Okay."

Endeara grinned, her teeth too much like a great white shark's choppers for my comfort. The witch's small, black eyes blinked slowly, reminding me of a reptile's gaze. Her pupils were tall and narrow like a reptile's too. Like the witches of human mythology, she had a long face with a sharply pointed chin. But her nose was...not a nose. It was more like two slits above a circular mouth that had trouble closing around all those teeth.

As silence stretched between us, I couldn't seem to stop myself from filling it. "So, this is the real you?"

Her grin widened. The too-sharp, jagged teeth were yellow, and the skin of her face was the color of pea soup.

I hated pea soup.

Endeara folded spidery fingers together in a plump lap and gave me a wink. "I know it's hard to accept that you're the ugly one in the room, Naida." She shrugged, her plump body vibrating under a laugh that sounded like a hysterical donkey braying. "But eat your heart out, dear."

"Heh," Bandy Joe said. "Good one." His voice was strained, and he had to clear it twice before he went on. "My understanding was that you'd seen the spirit of the piper," he told her. "Is that true?"

She shrugged. "I saw the shadow of the piper in a dream. That sometimes means the subject is dead. Sometimes not." She slanted me a gaze. "In my dream he was unformed, hazy like a specter. Whatever his true form, the creature was restless and angry. I got the sense he was being stalked by someone...or something...and wasn't happy about it."

"Are you saying he's being compelled?" Bandy Joe asked.

Endeara shrugged. "It's hard to say."

What she said made sense. I'd been trying to come up with a reason for what the piper had done in Enchanted. If he was being spurred on by a feeling of righteous anger, we might have some luck stopping him if we could figure out what caused it. "You don't know what's driving him?"

"I can make a guess." When I nodded, she went on. "He was very angry when he was cheated of his payment by the city of Hamelin. Very angry. Mythology is vague on what happened after the piper led the children away, as well as what happened to him later. But we do know that his rage was never sated. It's possible he's looking to reclaim his honor now."

I frowned. "But why us? Why Enchanted?"

The witch stared at me for a long moment. When she spoke, her words confused rather than clarified. "Are you aware of the theory of dimensional crimping?"

I shook my head. "I know about dimensional wrinkles. Are those the same thing?"

"No," Endeara said, shaking her head. "A wrinkle is an interdimensional shift, comprising more than one dimension. Dimensional crimping involves only a single dimension. You see, individual planes morph and twist all the time. They move and bump against each other. Sometimes, they are forced to fold in on themselves, or crimp, for a time. It is possible that your little town is located in the exact dimensional spot now where Hamelin was when the Piper performed his service in the twelve hundreds."

I frowned. "But Hamelin was in Germany. Why wouldn't he return there?"

"Apples and oranges, dear. You're talking geographic location. I'm referring to dimensional position, which shifts and changes as the stratum flexes."

I thought about what she'd said. "So, right now, in the piper's mind, Enchanted is Hamelin?"

"Yes."

"How can we stop him?"

She laughed that strange braying laugh again. "You are getting ahead of yourself, dear. First, you must find him."

"Can you help us with that?" Joe asked, hope coloring his question.

"I can discern his future actions," she answered. "But I can't tell you where he is at this very moment."

"Would you do that, please?" Bandy Joe asked.

She lifted a hand, her ten-inch-long fingers ending with sharp black nails. Given their range of movement, the fingers appeared to have a dozen joints. They rolled and twisted, creating a scrying space on the air that thinned and cleared until it was completely transparent. I viewed the witch through the space as if it were a window made of milky glass.

She tucked a lank hunk of blue-green hair

behind one oversized ear, and her lips began to move. The scrying area she'd created filled with a grayish mist that began to roil and surge as the spell she was concocting grew.

The mist rose and sank. It sat like a bank of fluffy clouds at the bottom of the magic window, revealing a row of bobbing items along the bottom. Endeara finished her spell and looked at her handiwork, frowning.

"That's not quite right." She leaned forward and pursed her lips, blowing upon the scrying space. The clouds at the bottom stretched and blew away, revealing what had been bobbing beneath the mist.

Horror spun ice in my veins.

It was a view of the Pied Piper, leading a bunch of small children through what looked like the streets of Enchanted.

I tore my gaze from the picture. "Is that happening now?"

Endeara sighed. "No, dear. It's a foreshadowing of what is to come. The details might change, but the spirit beneath the viewing is clear. The piper will compel someone else in your little town if you don't stop him." Her frown deepened. "It does tell us one thing for certain. The Pied Piper is alive. And he's apparently up to his old tricks."

Bandy Joe leaned forward in his chair. "But his pipe is locked in my magic vault," he told the witch. "How is this possible?"

She shrugged. "There are others who can create an enthralling pipe."

Joe and I shared a horrified glance. "Others? As in more than one?" I asked.

Endeara eyed the image between us, her sickly green brow wrinkling in thought. "No. Not at this level. There is only one wizard who can create an artifact that can compel this many people."

"Where can we find him?" Bandy Joe asked.

I sent Joe a look, feeling the weight of our task. "I'm no longer sure finding the wizard is a good use of our time."

"Why not?"

"Because I'm guessing the piper is in Enchanted. Maybe we should just go back and look for him there. It would be more efficient."

"I beg to differ, dear," Endeara said. "The piper could be anywhere. On any dimension. He is not constrained by dimensional boundaries. It has something to do with his enthralling magics. He can compel physical as well as spiritual objects. In fact," she went on. "I believe that is why his appearance seems unfocused. I believe it's possible for the piper to exist physically on one plane while utilizing his compelling magics on another dimension."

Hope dropped into a puddle around my feet. How in the name of the goddess's favorite Saturday night undies were we going to find a creature who could exist anywhere while destroying lives in our dimension?

I looked at Joe. "You think this wizard knows where he is?"

"No," he replied, his bulging black gaze intense on mine. "But I believe he can find him. Or, at least, he can find the artifact."

I felt hope lifting its shiny head again. "He can track the pipe?"

"He should be able to. It's become standard practice over the millennia for magical artifact creators to not only sign their work but to also insert a location spell into them." His wide brow furrowed. "Unless the piper requested that the spell not be inserted."

"How strong a possibility is that?" I asked.

He shrugged. "Sixty forty. Most savvy magic users will demand a clean artifact. But occasionally, one will be distracted enough not to think of it. I believe it's worth checking out."

After giving his advice a moment's thought, I nodded. "Okay. We'll find the wizard." I sent the witch a sheepish glance. "I don't suppose you can tell us where to find the wizard?"

She laughed again. I shuddered at the feeling of biting ants crawling over my arms from the sound. "That's easy, dear. You already know where he is."

"I do?"

"Why yes," Endeara shoved the arms of her chair

and heaved her bulk upright. "He's in the void. In the same place where you put him."

It took a beat for her meaning to sink in. And, when it did, I cringed. "George."

Ugh! Of course, it would be him.

The enormous raven followed us almost all the way back to the spot where we'd walked into the trees. Its menacing presence would have bothered me much more if I wasn't so busy worrying about another faceoff with the wizard who'd nearly taken everything I loved away from me.

Sure, I'd accidentally sent him and his friend into the void. I could see why that would make him a little grumpy. But he'd tried to eat Mr. Wicked. Okay, technically, he hadn't tried to *eat* him. He'd implied it, though. And he'd told Sebille she looked like the product of a paint store explosion.

Heh.

Okay, that part was funny.

"What did you do to this wizard, anyway?" Joe asked. "You turned white when Endeara told us you had to find him."

"Meow," Mr. Wicked said by way of explanation. He snapped his tail in emphasis. He wasn't wrong.

I'd only done what I had to do. But what I'd done had really hacked the wizard off.

"Let's just say we got off on the wrong foot, and things went downhill from there."

He shook his head. "Wizards hold grudges."

"Meow." Wicked agreed.

"Somehow, I'm going to have to get him to help us," I said. Even to me, my tone sounded hopeless. There was no way in the goddess's time-traveling hot tub he was going to work with me. "I need to offer him something big enough to entice him to help."

"Like what?" Joe asked.

"I have no idea."

We stepped out of the trees and into the small clearing where the mirror had dumped us. I jolted to a stop. "How are we going to get back?"

Bandy Joe gave me a sly smile. He reached into his pocket and gently extracted something small and bright blue. The tiny frog stared at me through bulgy orange eyes, its throat distending and shrinking in a lazy rhythm. Joe crooned to the little guy, carefully plucking pocket lint from its teensy paws.

"Um, Joe?"

He lifted the tiny creature to eye height on the palm of his hand. "Meet Zoom."

"Hey, Zoom." I waggled my fingers at the frog.

Bandy Joe reached into his other pocket and pulled out a sliver of glass. I recognized it as part of my communicating mirror, and my brows arched in understanding. "You brought a piece of the mirror. Smart."

"And an engine to get us started." He lifted the frog to indicate he was referring to him.

"Ribbit!" Zoom responded.

Joe set Zoom atop the glass and offered me his arm. "Ready?" Silvery Keeper's energy was already swirling around his hands.

"Wait!" I said.

He blinked in surprise and waited.

"Do you want to go home?" I asked. "I know you have your own life to get back to."

His smile widened. "Not a chance. I'm enjoying myself too much. Leandra is feeding the frogs and watching the store. Everything's taken care of. Let's go find us a Pied Piper."

I scooped up Wicked and took Joe's arm. "Let's do it."

Silvery magic slipped from Joe's fingers and swirled around Zoom and the sliver of glass. A moment later, we were ripped from the Enchanted Woods and flung through dimensional space, landing hard on the floor of Croakies. I hit first, landing flat on my stomach and shooting like a rocket across the room. Wicked left me with a yowl and skittered to safety beneath the desk.

I was heading toward the dividing door and couldn't stop myself, reaching it just as Hobs threw the door open. The heavy wood smacked me right in the face. Stars burst before my eyes, even before I slammed into the wall behind it.

Joe did a controlled roll in front of the broken mirror, his pudgy body wrapped protectively around Zoom, and jumped to his feet.

Groaning miserably, I lay behind the door, my lips smashed against the floor and my body sprawled in an ungainly mess.

"Sorry, Miss," Hobs said, crouching down beside me. He laid a warm hand against my back. "Are you okay?"

I tried to lift my head and a tooth fell out, rolling across the floor. "Um," I moved a leg, and something in my back cracked like window-glass in a rock storm. "Ah." Even my hair hurt. "Ugh."

"Miss?" Hobs sounded even more worried.

"What happened to her?" a soft voice asked. Another small body crouched next to me. A second small hand joined Hobbs's hand on my back. Bacca, the brownie, rubbed my back in gentle circles. "Is she alive?"

I groaned.

Bandy Joe's shoes appeared near my head. "Shall I get the sprite?"

I tried to lift my head, but something in my neck creaked when I moved. I went very still, afraid my spine would crack and my head would fall off. "Pleath," I said through the hole where my tooth had been.

"Poor, Miss," breathed Baca. "I need to fix her."

"No!" I shouted before I could stop myself. The tiny hand on my back hesitated. "I mean. Thank you, Baca. I appreciate everything you do around Croakies. But Sebille knows how to help me. Thank you so much, though."

The small hand lifted, and she stood. I tried to sit up, but nothing was working. Plus, I had some weird throbbing along the center of my face, and I was pretty sure my nose had already swollen to the size of a plum. "Why don't you two go fetch Sebille for me? That would be a big help."

They scooted away amid peals of happy giggling.

I sighed and sagged downward.

"Brownies are sensitive, I guess," Bandy Joe said.

"Very. At least this one is. She wants to help so badly, but she doesn't understand the difference between fixing a chair and fixing a body. Last week she tried to heal a paper cut on my thumb and ended up giving me three thumbs on that hand. Sebille tried everything to fix it, but we ended up calling Dr. Whom."

Joe nodded. "She's a lovely creature."

I smiled. "She is. And very sweet. Hobs is crazy about her."

Something must have come through in my voice because Joe said. "And that's bad?"

I sighed, immediately regretting it when another tooth flew out of my head. "Not bad, exactly..."

"But you're worried she'll break his heart?"

"Yeah. I'm not proud of it. But I am."

"You need to trust the little guy, Naida. He's not stupid."

"No. He's not stupid at all. Well, except about flinging himself into walls. He's pretty stupid about that."

Bandy Joe chuckled. "Trust the brownie too. From everything I've ever heard about them, they're very conscientious and extremely hard workers."

"Right again," I admitted. Sighing, I said. "Let's think about something easier." I cranked my eye around so I could look at him. "You realize we're going to have to go into the void, right?"

To my shock, Joe clapped his hands together in glee. "I do. And I can't wait. I've never actually gone into the void before."

Heavy footsteps pounded toward us from across the artifact library. Sebille was on her way.

She arrived pink-cheeked and panting. "The kids told me you were in pieces on the floor."

I tried to laugh, but something creaked loudly in my knee, so I stopped. "They weren't wrong."

She bent over me, running her hands along my sprawled form, trying to assess the damage. Then she sat back on her heels. "Other than your face, which might be a lost cause, it's not as bad as it looks. We'll have you fixed up in no time."

She looked at Bandy Joe. "Hi."

"Hi, Sebille. You look winded."

She nodded. "I was over at the greenhouse, visiting with my mother."

"Why didn't you sprout wings?" I asked her. In her sprite form, she whipped around with minimal expenditure of energy and covered ground a lot faster, despite her dragonfly-sized body.

She flushed pink again, and her gaze skimmed away from mine. No snarky response. No yelling.

Alarm bells rang in my head. Something was wrong.

I realized I hadn't seen her go small for a few days. I opened my mouth to ask, but she slammed her palms onto my back and sent a raging inferno of healing heat into my flesh.

After that, there was just a lot of screaming and whining for the next hour.

Yeah, unfortunately it was me doing all the screaming and whining. I'm not proud of it.

7

IT WAS RECKLESS OF HIM TO BREATHE SO LOUD LIKE THAT

"Why don't you pop into a bug and head back to grab Blackbeard's sword off the top shelf for me." I watched the sprite carefully for a reaction.

She rolled her eyes—not an unexpected response coming from her. "We need to talk about how we're going to handle the wizard."

I sipped the tea she'd made me, pretending I wasn't worried about our upcoming outing to the void. "I want to ask Archie to come."

"Why?" she asked, narrowing her gaze.

"He's the king of the voids."

"He's a void sorcerer. That hardly makes him a king."

"Is there a reason you don't want him to come?" I asked.

She shrugged. "I just think we'll have a better shot if we travel small. In and out, really fast."

I grabbed the opening. "Speaking of traveling small..."

The dividing door opened. Bandy Joe came through. He had a frog on his shoulder like a tiny, orange-eyed parrot. "I found it," he told us, referring to the Book of Pages I'd misplaced somewhere in the library. The book was a handy way to move around the earthly dimension and possibly other dimensions as well. But the one and only time we'd used it for cross-dimensional travel, we'd created a hole into the void, and you don't even want to know what happened after that.

Okay, you probably do. All I'm going to say is monsters. Lots of monsters. The result had been lots of messy monster mashing and a broken book store. I was also pretty sure the event had given me Book of Pages PTSD since I kept inadvertently misplacing it.

Sebille headed for the front door. "I'll be back. I have an errand."

"Wait!" I demanded.

As usual, she ignored me. But she didn't get far. Opening the front door, the sprite jolted to a stop to avoid running into Rustin. His hand out as if to grasp the knob, he blinked in surprise. "Hey."

Sadie flew past him and into the store, buzzing up to the top of the bookshelves in search of her friends, the songbirds. I'm happy to say the noisy creatures were all gone, and Hobbs had been banned from using the magical hand-vac that had created them.

When the little dragon saw there were no friends singing from the shelves, she buzzed back to Rustin and landed on his outstretched palm. Sadie warbled softly, her slanted eyes turning turquoise for a moment and then going black again. "Where are you off to so fast?" Rustin asked my assistant, moving past her into the store.

"She's avoiding me," I said, hands on hips. I needed her to admit she was having a problem so we could figure out how to fix it. A sprite that couldn't flash into her natural form was in danger. Their magic was strongest in their dragonfly-sized form. She was also better able to avoid danger in that form, a fact that had saved her and me more than once.

"Stop talking," the sprite barked at me before hurrying out the door.

I stared after her, chewing my bottom lip with worry.

"What's up with her?" Rustin asked.

I took a deep breath and expelled it. "I'm not sure. But I'm going to find out."

He nodded. "I came to ask if you need help in the void?"

My eyes went round. "You and Sadie are willing to come?"

"Of course. It's been a little boring around here

lately." The twitching of his lips told me he was being funny.

"Yeah. I can see how turning into an ancient mythological creature would be dry as toast."

Rustin was dual-natured, meaning he had a human and an animal form. I used to call him a ghost witch because he'd lost his corporeal form due to an unfortunate family spell. Long story short, he'd needed a body after his evil uncle Jacob Quilleran put his soul into a frog, specifically *my* frog Slimy. Rustin's aunt Madeline had given him shifter DNA so he'd have a body again. His second nature was a chimera, half-lion, and half-dragon. We'd only recently met his terrifying but beautiful new form when he'd nearly eaten a couple of nasty cherubs and Grym.

Another long story. Suffice it to say that he'd truly earned the new moniker, shifter witch.

Rustin gave up trying to hold back a grin. "I was actually thinking more along the lines of you and Sebille marrying those ogres."

I glared his way.

Bandy Joe held his hand out to Rustin. "Hello. I'm Joe."

Rustin took the offered hand. "Rustin. It's nice to meet you."

Joe nodded. "Naida has talked about you. It's a pleasure."

Rustin glanced at me, peaking one dark brow in question.

"Bandy Joe and I met during the coin-hoarding case." That had been the first time I'd traveled to Joe's version of Croakies. We'd been chasing a gold-coin-making artifact that had already caused a couple of deaths and was on track to cause many more. Involving giant stink bugs, deadly dragons, and a particularly poisonous artifact, it had been quite an adventure.

"Ah," Rustin grinned. "That one sounded like fun."

"It's never boring around Naida," Joe agreed.

"Isn't that the truth?"

"Says the man who turns into a chimera," I said, glaring at him.

"Really?" Joe bounced with excitement. "I'd like to see that."

"No," I said. "You wouldn't. He almost ate the last guy who got too close."

"That's not fair," Rustin told the sprite. "Grym antagonized me when I wasn't at my best."

"Absolutely," I agreed. "It was reckless of him to breathe so loud like that."

Rustin shook his head.

The front door opened, and Sebille came back inside. I glanced at the sprite. She determinedly avoided my gaze, placing a large, greasy sack on the table.

My eyes went wide. "Is that what I think it is?" My mouth was already watering.

She went into the tea area and came back with a pile of napkins. "We'll need our strength if we're going to play whack-a-wizard."

Joe's nostrils flared. "Is that?"

Rustin moved on the bag, a gleam in his gaze.

Sebille snatched it out of his path before he could grab it. "You don't get first dibs. You'll take too many."

Rustin tried to look innocent, but nobody was buying the act. It was a tough audience. "Have a heart, Sebille. Do you know how hard it was to watch you two eat those things as a bodiless spirit?"

Rustin had still been in his ghost-witch form when Sebille and I had gone to a Chinese restaurant to interview a suspect. At the time, he'd acted like he didn't care we were stuffing our faces with egg rolls. Clearly, he'd been covering up his real feelings.

"That was one time," she said, tugging a small wax bag out of the larger bag. "You need to let that go."

"I could smell them," he whined. "Do you know what it's like to smell egg rolls and not eat any?"

Sebille nodded. "I do. Which is why I'm not letting you dive in here first." She handed me the bag, and I plucked a small wax bag with two fat egg rolls out of it. "Oh my gosh!" I said, moaning. "These do smell incredible." I plucked a roll from the bag and stuffed it into my mouth. Then, I made the mistake of looking at Rustin.

He was giving me softer eyes than even Sadie managed. And that was saying something. With a long-suffering sigh, I handed him the second roll in the bag.

Sebille shook her head. "Sucker."

I grabbed the bag and dug a serving out for Bandy Joe. "Guilty as charged."

The front door slammed open, and we all turned to find a large man with mahogany brown hair and dark caramel eyes staring at us.

We all continued to chew.

"How'd you smell them all the way out on the street?" Sebille asked, disgusted.

Grym moved swiftly forward, grabbing the bag before Sebille could pull it away from him.

She stuffed the last bite of her first egg roll into her mouth and sighed, heading for the door. "I'll be back," she said around the bite of egg roll.

We barely heard her as we dove on the bag like dragons on a pile of gold.

"We need weapons," Rustin said, frowning. "I remember what you told me about those wizards from the last time."

Grym shook his head. "We can't just go into the void and start attacking them."

"Why not?" Sebille asked. "You don't think they'll attack us first?"

He nodded, his expression annoyingly reasonable. "I have no doubt they will. But a dead wizard can't help us with our problem, can he?"

The room went silent as we all considered that.

Finally, Sebille said, "What about if we just maim him a lot?"

Bandy Joe snorted. "The biggest danger we have from these guys is their fire magic, right?"

The last time we'd faced off with them, the two wizards we'd trapped in the void had sent a flood of bubbling, black acid through the void, which ate its way through everything it touched. It had been a miracle we weren't melted on the spot.

"What artifacts do we have that might combat that?" Rustin asked.

I thought about it. "I'll have to research it. Off the top of my head, I can't think of anything."

"What about Brad Spence?" Grym asked.

I blinked in surprise. "Brad?"

"Oh!" Sebille said, her face lighting up. "The Phoenix shifter. Of course." She looked at me. "He'd be perfect."

I thought about the suggestion for a minute. Brad had once saved me from a wizard's ugly black magic by literally eating the stuff while in his

Phoenix form. He'd also helped out with some spilled toxic magic once. Being a fireman, I know, ironic, Brad was a handy guy to have around.

But he wasn't one of us.

"I was hoping to keep this small and friendly...if you know what I mean." I really hoped they did because I didn't want to explain why we were entering the void to shake down a wizard for information to anyone outside our little group. The Pied Piper struck fear into the hearts of the supernormal community like no other. The idea of losing control of personal will was terrifying.

Grym looked like he was going to argue, but my phone rang. I held up a finger to stop him and answered. "This is Naida."

"Naida, keeper," a gravelly voice bellowed.

I pulled the phone from my ear. Which was okay because I didn't need to hold the phone that close to hear King Rhorr's thundering voice.

"Get over here right now. One of my people has died. I'm going to find that piper and tear him to shreds!"

The call disconnected before I could respond. "I have to go see the ogres," I said, quickly filling them in on what the king had screamed into my ear.

"I'll go with you," Grym said.

Grym drove because he insisted. I was okay with that for two reasons. One, his heavy black car was much more intimidating than my cute little beetle bug. And two, he was a cop and therefore able to go faster than I could.

Also, the sprite and Bandy Joe fit better into the back seat of his car. Though, I would have welcomed the opportunity to nudge Sebille into going buggy again if we'd taken my car.

I was really glad we'd brought the intimidating vehicle when we arrived at Rhorr's kingdom. A large contingent of ogres met us there, lined up behind their king in long but surprisingly tidy rows.

Every ogre's face was dark with a rage that mirrored their king's. There would be no cheerful bantering or playful Naida-squishing.

I glanced at Grym, and he gave me back a stony expression. "This is going to be very delicate," he said. He looked at me, but I knew his message was for everyone. "Let me do the talking."

Nobody argued. There were hundreds of ogres lined up across the rocky land. Like their king, they tended to have very short fuses. Judging from the encounters we'd already had with them, we'd be lucky to defeat *one* of them in a hand-to-hand battle. The numbers we were facing would easily pound us into dust at their king's feet.

"Rhorr is the key," I told him. "We need to convince him that we can fix this."

Grym nodded, and we all piled out of the car. I turned to Sebille. "Maybe you should make like a wasp and rise above the situation. Just in case we need back up."

She glowered and stepped around me, her stride stiff and angry. I stared after her a moment, my minor worry blossoming into real concern. Something was terribly wrong with the sprite.

I needed to stop getting distracted and find out what it was.

I strode after the others, falling in beside Bandy Joe. He nudged me with an elbow, drawing my gaze down to a tiny book sitting on his palm. It was The Book of Pages. He'd shrunk it to its travel size. "I thought you might want a Plan B."

Relief filled me. I didn't really think Rhorr's people would attack us...hopefully...but it was good to have an exit plan just in case. "Good thinking." I took the book and wrapped my fingers around it. I'd keep it in my hand for faster access.

Grym stopped six feet away from the king. He was close enough to show we weren't afraid of the irate ruler but far enough away to have some maneuvering room if we needed it.

"King Rhorr." He inclined his head in greeting. "We've come as you requested. Please tell us what happened."

The king had completed the transformation to a stiff and unyielding ruler whose last ounce of patience had been stripped away. His big fists were clenched, the knuckles white, and behind the intractable rage in his brittle blue gaze was the merest touch of fear that sent ice skittering through me. "One of our most cherished elders has died from the attack of the pied demon. This outrage will not go unanswered."

He drew himself up, his black velvet robes swirling around his thick legs with the movement. "I have called you here to give notice. I, Ogre King Rhorr, declare that my kingdom is under siege. It is my unhappy duty to inform you that I am declaring a state of war."

8

DON'T. CALL. ME. EVER. AGAIN.

Grym paled to an unhealthy vanilla ice cream color. "King Rhorr..."

The angry ruler held up a hand, palm out. "You do not have a say in my decisions. My people have been attacked, and it cannot stand."

"But it's one man, sir," Grym tried again. "What you're proposing will cost too many lives."

"Silence!" Rhorr bellowed. His face was purple, his bulbous nose an alarming shade of burgundy, and his eyes beamed blue fire at Grym.

Lifting his hands in surrender, Grym lowered his head in an effort to calm the king.

A large, warm hand found my shoulder. I looked up into a terrified purple gaze.

Maxine leaned close, her lips mere inches from my ear. She whispered more softly than I thought was possible for an ogre. "Ask to see Mama Theresa."

I frowned, opening my mouth to ask for clarification. But Maxine's hand squeezed my shoulder, and I almost went down to my knees from the pain. My mouth opened in a silent scream. I caught the king looking at me, his bushy white brows lowered over the blue beads of his eyes.

"I..." I said, twisting out of Maxine's grip. "I was wondering..." I rolled my shoulder and gave her a glare. She looked back at me with such innocence that nobody would guess she'd nearly broken my bones. "...if I could see Mama Theresa."

The king's bushy brows lifted slightly. He stared at me for a long moment and then nodded. "You and Sebille only. No-one outside the family."

Grym looked like he would argue, but I gave him a quick shake of my head. He backed down but didn't look happy.

Maxine limped along with us to the portal which would take us to the king's royal cave.

As we walked, the crowd turned and followed, the long lines of angry ogres moving in a surprisingly cohesive way. My heart sank as I realized they looked just like an army on the march.

The front line bulged and Rick emerged, moving to walk behind Sebille as Maxine walked behind me. They were apparently our buffer against the madding crowd.

It made me feel marginally better.

The king stepped into the portal and was engulfed in a shimmery, gelatinous substance that quickly folded over him, hiding him from sight.

Sebille and I stepped through together. As before, the cool, pseudo-slimy feel of the portal was disconcerting. But experience had taught me just to move through it with calm, determined steps rather than try to hurry or shove my way through. As a result, Sebille and I stepped out into King Rhorr's throne room without incident. Unlike the time we'd both landed in his lap from an overzealous trip through the goo.

The space was unchanged except for the addition of an enormous table in the center. The walls and thirty-foot high ceilings were carved from natural rock, and the floor was a mixture of hard dirt and stone. At the back of the space, a single passage had been hewn from the mountain. I'd never been down that passageway. But the last time I'd been there, Rhorr had emerged from it holding a sandwich. So I presumed it led to some kind of kitchen at the very least.

As far as furnishings, a thick, deep-red rug with gold tassels sat beneath the king's throne, and there were a few massive chairs positioned around the walls.

Rhorr's throne was not in its customary spot in the center. In its place was a long table carved of rock. Lying on top of the table, on a gold and burgundy pad fit for a queen, lay the ogre I assumed was Mama Theresa. She was dressed in a frothy white gown, her bony arms crossed on her chest, and flowers had been braided into her long, silvery-white hair. Her features were large, her color a soft gray, and her eyes were open, frosted with death.

I fought a grimace.

Maxine must have noticed. She moved up next to me and spoke in low tones. "We leave the eyes open so the dead can find their way to utopia." She nodded to the large, bony feet beneath the gown. "We leave their feet dusty and bare, so they may bathe them in the silver waters of paradise." She walked over and touched an age-freckled hand with gentle reverence, lifting it to show me a single gold coin. "We send them away with riches to ensure they make an easy path."

I nodded, strangely touched by their reverential grieving practices.

"This woman..." King Rhorr began, his voice husky with emotion. "...was a treasure to my people. Do you know how long she has walked in this world?"

I shook my head.

"Four hundred years," he said, biting off each word. He placed a gentle hand over hers. "For four centuries, she has been our touchstone, our historian, our calm voice, and our stiff spine. She has loved the world, been broken by it more than once, and has cloaked herself in a resilient spirit to embrace it again and again." His strong voice broke, and he cleared his throat, the sound harsh in the otherwise silent space. "Her loss is like having our collective hearts ripped right out of our chests."

Behind me, Rick and Maxine both sniffed wetly. On an impulse, I reached over and clasped Maxine's hand, giving it a squeeze. She looked away, scrubbing at tears with obvious embarrassment.

"That is why..." Rhorr continued. "I have no choice but to avenge her death." He fixed me with a hard blue gaze. "Blood will spill in the streets of Enchanted until I have the culprit of her senseless death in my grip."

"King Rhorr..."

His beady gaze flashed rage in my direction.

I swallowed hard and inclined my chin. "My deepest condolences."

Sebille muttered commiserations to join mine.

"Surely you see that harming the innocent people of Enchanted won't help the situation in any way?"

There was a burst of light, and I found myself blinking at a tiny form hanging in the air in front of me. The pixie's enormous moth-like wings undulated on the air like an airborne manta ray.

The tiny, puckish face frowned in my direction. The famous Shirley of "don't call me Shirley" stared daggers at me. She opened her mouth to yell at me for calling her, but Sebille gave her head a quick shake. Apparently a quick study, the pixie swung her gaze around the room, widening at the sight of the dead ogre and a stone-faced King Rhorr. She did a quick curtsy on the air. "Your majesty."

"Out," Rhorr barked.

Panicked, Shirley spun around in a full circle, her wings beating the air double-time, and disappeared in a flash of painful light, leaving behind a whisper on the air for my ears only.

Don't. Call. Me. Ever. Again.

"Sorry, King Rhorr," I said. "A slip of the tongue."

He shook his head. "That pixie is nasty. She's been banished from my kingdom several times. She should have known better."

She probably couldn't resist another chance to take a shot at me. "As I was saying, can I suggest an alternative to war?" When he growled, I shook my head. "Just a temporary cease-fire. If I can't find this guy in a week, you can do what you need to do."

He arched a bushy white brow. "*Can* I?"

Babbling baby buzzards! I felt as if I was walking across a minefield. "Of course, you don't need my permission..."

The other brow lifted, and I was pretty sure blue flames were about to shoot from his eyes.

I made a time-out motion with my hands. "Look, all I'm asking is for a little time before you do what you want to do. The guy's using an artifact. I'm an artifact keeper. It's my responsibility to stop him and lock that artifact up. I have family and friends in Enchanted. My store is there. I don't want to see you flatten the town and hurt all those people. Do you understand?"

Amazingly, his expression did soften. He narrowed his eyes thoughtfully and then jerked his head toward the portal entrance.

For a moment, I thought he was throwing the sprite and me out on our ears. But he looked at the ogres hulking behind us. "Leave us!" he commanded.

I swallowed hard and glanced at Sebille. She didn't dismiss his antics with a roll of her eyes, which scared me more than my own misgivings. And when Maxine and Rick hesitated, I knew we were in trouble. "King Rhorr..."

He stabbed a finger at me, and I clamped my lips shut.

I caught Maxine's eye and gave her a pleading look. She visibly winced but turned and left.

There was a long moment of silence before the king spoke again. When he did, his voice was strained, the words soft. "I do not want a war, Naida keeper."

I blinked in surprise, not sure what to say. So I simply nodded.

He expelled a long breath, rubbing his hands

over his face. For a moment, he turned to look at the woman on the table. "I will greatly miss her love and guidance."

It occurred to me that the dead woman might be more to Rhorr than he'd implied. Could she have been his mother? I looked at Mama Theresa again. Or grandmother?

"I will absolve you of your contractual obligations."

I jolted, my gaze flying back to him. "Excuse me?"

Rhorr fixed a sad smile on his face and skimmed it over Sebille and me. "If you bring this man to me within three days, you will not have to marry my ogres."

My lips flapped like a trout in the grass. Fortunately, Sebille spoke up. Finally. "Majesty, Naida can't turn him over to you."

"Why not?"

"Her job is to get the artifact..."

His smile brightened. "Excellent. Then take the artifact and call me in to deal with the monster who killed Mama Theresa."

"That's Grym's job," I forced myself to say. "I'm sorry, but I can't be part of vigilante justice. Grym will imprison the Pied Piper, and the creature will be charged for his crimes by the PTB. Then he will go before the Société of Dire Magic for trial. It's the way it has to be."

Rhorr looked honestly confused. "Why?"

"Imagine if every supernormal clan took things into their own hands. It would be chaos. The world wouldn't be safe for anyone."

He puffed up, straightening to his full eight-feet-plus height. "I am not just any supernormal. I am king."

I stared at him for a long moment.

He finally deflated a little, nodding. "Very well. Detective Grym may take the man to be tried. I only request the opportunity to speak to the Société before he is tried."

"I'm sure that can be arranged."

"If you do not capture the man within three days, the wedding will be in one month."

And with those words, my stomach clenched tighter than Shirley the Pixie's anus.

9

YOUR DIMENSION IS REALLY STRESSFUL

"We need to leave for the void tonight," I told Grym and Bandy Joe in a near whisper.

His head on a wary swivel, Grym was staying close behind us, basically herding us forward as we moved quickly but carefully off the King's property. We were surrounded on three sides by ogres who'd apparently taken it upon themselves to make sure we left. Their expressions were taut with rage, and I couldn't help feeling as if the smallest thing might set them off.

"We'll discuss it when we get out of here," Grym said, his tone a quiet warning.

I looked at Sebille. "What was with you in there? You barely said two words."

Sebille glared over at me. "Stop talking."

I bit back a retort. I knew they were right. Bickering between the four of us was the perfect spark to turn the group behind us into a raging mob.

By the time we reached the parking lot and climbed into Grym's big car, I was covered in flop sweat and was pretty sure I'd fractured a couple of teeth from clenching my jaw.

Nobody spoke until we were a few miles down the road. Then we all took a deep breath and released it, expelling some of the tension.

"Your dimension is really stressful," Bandy Joe said, mopping his wide brow with his sleeve.

I barked out a laugh. "Yes, it is. I need a vacation." Or some sleep. Sleep would be really nice.

Grym's expression was tight, his eyes hard. I reached across the car and touched his arm. "What's wrong?"

He finally looked at me. "You can't let them force that marriage."

"Marriage?" Bandy Joe sounded shocked and appalled in equal measure. "What marriage?"

I turned in my seat and looked at Sebille, expecting her to pipe in. But she was staring out the window with a murderous look on her long, freckled face. "Sebille? What's going on with you?"

The sprite acted as if I hadn't spoken. "Sebille!"

I'd hoped yelling her name would surprise her out of her funk, but she kept her gaze on the window and said, "Leave it be, Naida."

"I mean it, Naida," Grym said, his tone bordering

on frantic. "I know I've been making fun of this whole marriage thing. But I just realized how dangerous this situation is for you two. We need to find a way to get you and Sebille out of it."

"Will somebody please tell me what's going on?" Joe said. He looked from me to Sebille and back to me again, his eyebrows lifting in question.

"We made a mistake," I told him, my eyes locked on the sprite. "We signed an ogrish contract without reading the fine print."

His eyes went wide. "Oh, oh."

"Yeah."

"You know there's no way out of those, don't you?"

Sebille finally turned her head, her iridescent green gaze finding mine. She gave her head a tiny shake, and I interpreted that to mean she didn't want me to tell them what Rhorr had said. I frowned, not understanding. Why wouldn't we tell Grym?

She shook her head again, her glower deepening.

Finally, I said, "I know. We're working on it."

"We need to work harder," Grym said. "You can't go through with it, Naida."

I turned back to him, the look of pure terror on his handsome face taking me by surprise. He quickly hid it, turning away to watch the road as we crossed the Enchanted town limits. "If we need to escape to another dimension, you're not fulfilling that contract."

His words smacked me in the chest like a bullet. It hadn't really hit me until that moment what Rhorr had signed us up for. Or rather, what we'd signed ourselves up for by being negligent. I realized I'd been as guilty as Grym of taking it too lightly. I'd never really believed it was going to happen. Somewhere in the back of my mind, I'd assumed we'd find a way to get out of the contract. But I'd been wrong. The obligation was a hard, dangerous reality. Ogres were a tight-knit clan. As a group, they hated and distrusted outsiders. I thought about how quickly they'd turned on us back there. Being around them was dangerous.

I reached over and squeezed Grym's hand. "We're going to work it out," I told him, my tone more confident than it should have been.

"How?" he asked, stopping the car in front of Croakies and killing the engine. "Joe's right. There's no way out of those contracts. If you fail to keep your end, the ogres will kill you. It's not a doable option."

Sweat ran down my back, and I longed for a hot shower. "I have an idea. We're going to work it out. Okay?"

He reached out and took my hand, kissing the back. "I'll do anything I can. Do you want me to go see Madeline?"

Madeline Quilleran, Rustin's aunt, was the PTB

representative for the earthly dimension. She might be able to lobby the Universal Council about making Rhorr retract the contract.

They were the only ones he might respect enough to listen to.

"I don't think that will be necessary."

"But..."

The back door slammed hard enough to shake the car. I turned to see Sebille stalking into the store.

"What's wrong with her?" Grym asked.

I shook my head, not bothering to hide my concern from him. "I don't know. But I need to find out. Preferably before we bring her into the void with us."

Sebille was standing in front of Shakespeare's desk, her hands clenched into fists at her sides. Her long, vibrantly red hair flew around her head is if caught in a windstorm. For the first time, I noticed how rumpled she looked. Her loose-fitting, purple dress was bunched around the waistline as if she'd been clutching at it. One of her striped socks had crumpled around her ankle, half-covering one of her Wicked Witch of the West shoes. Her waist-length hair was loose instead of in its usual braids.

She trembled violently from head to toe.

I closed the dividing door and stood there, waiting. She knew I was there. She knew why. It would be up to her to talk to me.

It didn't take long.

"I've always hated my heritage," she said, her voice so soft I found myself leaning forward to hear it. "I was embarrassed by it. Rebelled against it by spending most of my time in human form." She winced as if disgusted with herself.

Lifting a quaking hand, the sprite tucked hair behind a pointed ear before going on. "I guess it's like anything else. You don't know what you have... until it's gone."

She left that bombshell sitting between us for a beat.

I suddenly found it hard to breathe. Panic clutched at my lungs with rabid fingers. I swallowed hard and took a deep breath before speaking. "Gone?"

She nodded. After a beat, she turned to me, her vibrant green gaze filled with pain. "I can't shift into my fairy form, Naida."

"Why?" I shook my head. "Scratch that. Do you know what happened?"

Her flat chest rose in a deep breath. "I can guess. I think it's stress."

"Over the wedding mess?"

She nodded. "I've seen mother's healers. They've

done tests, given me elixirs, and pelted me with spells. Nothing fixes it."

"Have you talked to Lea about it?"

She looked at the floor, her throat working over the emotions she was battling. "No. I'm...embarrassed."

"Embarrassed? Because we didn't dive into the king's buttcrack to read the fine print?"

She snorted out a laugh and then hugged herself. "That was a nasty trick to put the fine print there."

"Yes, it was. But there was a certain evil genius to it."

We'd gone to the ogre king for a special type of artifact to help us solve a particularly difficult mystery. They would only let us lease the artifact, which required us to sign a contract. A contract that was written on the naked king's broad back. The fine print was in a spot far below where we wanted to read...if you catch my meaning. I'll admit it, Sebille and I had wimped out. We'd signed the contract magically, from a safe distance, without reading the fine print.

It was only later that we'd discovered what that fine print had said. We were engaged to two ogres. Maxine and Rick.

She turned to me. "Do you think he'll really give us an out if we find the piper?"

"I do." King Rhorr was many things, but he

wasn't dishonest. He'd helped us many times already, and he'd always kept his end of the bargain. "We're going to find him, Sebille. And then your stress will disappear. You'll be fine."

"I hope you're right," she said, not sounding like she believed me.

"I am." Then, I did something I don't think I'd ever done before. I pulled the sprite into a hug, holding her tightly even when she didn't return the embrace. "It's going to work out, Sebille. I feel it in my heart."

After a long moment, she finally wrapped her skinny arms around me and held on tight.

Really, painfully tight. For a very long time.

———

We stood in a tight circle in the middle of Croakies. I held the Book of Pages out in front of me. Sebille, Grym, Bandy Joe, and Rustin each placed their fingers on the book.

Sebille refused to look at me, no doubt embarrassed by her show of neediness from earlier. She prided herself on being stronger than everyone else. More competent. It probably only added to her stress to discover she was fallible too.

"Is everybody ready?"

Heads bobbed around me. I ignored the pinched

aspect of all their faces and cleared my mind so I could direct us to the right place in the void. That was going to be tricky enough, given that everything there was mixed up and amorphous.

The pages of the book began to flip, searching for the spot where we wanted to go. It continued to flip, waiting for me to give it the location. But, before I could picture the right spot in my mind, worry crept in. My face must have shown my confusion.

"What?" Grym asked.

"Huh?"

"Why did you just pucker up like a giant's anus?" Sebille asked.

I grimaced. "Ew."

She shrugged, and her vibrant green gaze caught mine. I was happy to see a little of the old Sebille shining back at me in those eyes.

"I was just wondering if it's a mistake not to bring the Phoenix."

"I can still call him," Grym offered, reaching for his cell.

Apparently, I wasn't the only one having second thoughts about that. But we'd decided that a smaller group was better. And we thought we had an alternative option to keep the wizard from transforming into a black, oily puddle on us. I glanced at the colorful lei clutched in Sebille's hand.

The flowers were real, but they never died or wilted unless they were doing their job. Rustin had come up with the idea when researching Sadie's home in Hawaii. Born in a world of erupting volcanos and boiling lava, the magic lei was made to lock the wearer away from the fire element. The best part was that it worked both ways. The wearer also couldn't use a heat element.

But there was a catch. We had to get the lei around the wizard's neck. And we had to do it before he turned completely into oily black lava and cooked us into steaming smudges.

The sweet scent of the flowers wafted over me, and something clicked inside my brain.

"No. This is right." I nodded decisively and closed my eyes, picturing the image of the last place we'd seen the wizard in the void. I felt the magic take hold a heartbeat later. A beat after that, it yanked me off the ground and whipped me into a cyclone of frantic magical energy, ripping me out of my world and dumping me moments later into the place of nightmares.

10

HOW ARE THINGS IN PARADISE?

My feet hit the ground just as thunder rolled over us, and I fell to my knees onto rocky ground that was black and sharp and crumbled beneath my weight. I coughed as a wave of hot, sulfurous air slammed into me.

Around me, a chorus of similar choking coughs reminded me I wasn't alone. My gaze shot up, but the air was thick with smoke and I couldn't see anybody except Bandy Joe. He was sitting on the ground next to me, his eyes bulging even more than usual as he hacked and coughed and struggled to breathe. As I looked at him, the strands of his hair split apart at the top and a confused little face stared out at me. Zoom. He looked as distressed as his owner.

I grabbed Joe's arm, giving it a tug. "Come on, we need to get out of here."

He climbed slowly to his feet as I looked for the others.

"Over here!" Rustin called from somewhere behind me. I whipped around to find him standing on a small hill about a block away, Sadie buzzing nervously around him. The smoke that coated my lungs and stung my eyes hadn't spread to the little hill.

I grabbed Joe's arm and tugged him, pointing at Rustin.

Thunder roared through the area again, the ground quaking beneath us. I stumbled sideways, nearly falling, and bumped into Joe.

"Go!" I yelled at him. I'd spotted Grym. He was bent over, reaching into the thick haze. A beat later, he tugged Sebille to her feet. She looked green around the gills, and her luminous gaze was unnaturally wide. She was coughing so hard Grym had to support her as they made their way to me.

I reached for the lei and pulled it from her grip, dropping it unceremoniously over her head.

The sprite stopped coughing almost immediately, her breaths slowing.

A series of lessor rumbles rolled over us. I pointed to Rustin rather than try to shout over them. We lurched after Bandy Joe, Grym and I hacking our lungs up as we hit the hill. It had looked like a small rise from a distance, but still battling the smoke in my lungs, it felt as if I were climbing Mount Enchanted.

The lei dropped over my head, and the sun-warmed scent of flowers enveloped me. My lungs immediately cleared, and I could take a full breath again. I gave Sebille a nod of thanks. By the time we reached the top, I felt as good as new.

Well, except for the knives spearing my calves and thighs from climbing the hill. I really needed to get into better shape.

"What did you do?" Rustin asked. "Where is the Croakies mirror image?"

That was an excellent question. "I don't know," I admitted. "I just thought of the wizard in void-Croakies, and it brought us here." Had the lei been on my mind when I set our destination? That would certainly explain what we were seeing.

We all stared out at the unending charcoal land-scape. The only color in the bleak panorama came in the form of the gold and orange lava bubbling out of an honest to goddess volcano. The boiling rock poured down the side of the huge, flat-topped mountain, sizzling along the ground at the bottom and cooling to the crunchy black rock we'd landed on.

"How are we going to find the wizard?" Sebille asked.

Sadie gave a chirp and flew circles around us. Her eyes glowed with aqua light. The illumination sifted along her body, fading to white as it slid off the tip of her tail and flashed like a warning beacon through the shadowy atmosphere.

She was chittering wildly, her eyes flashing different colors with every throb of her wings.

"What's she saying?" I asked Sebille, who, for some unknown reason could understand the tiny dragon's gibberish.

"There's somebody here," Sebille said, frowning. "In the lava."

"In the lava?" Grym asked, frowning.

"That's not possible," Joe said.

"Have you ever dealt with a wizard?" I asked the other keeper, my gaze locked on the scene below us.

"Fortunately, no. I understand they're a nasty bunch."

"That's an understatement," Grym said. "They can dissolve themselves into rivers of black acid that melt flesh and bone."

Joe winced. "Sounds like fun."

Rustin's hand came up, pointing to a spot in the cooling rock that had bulged outward, like a giant boil on the surface of the rock. "What's happening there?"

The boil grew and stretched, assuming a vaguely man-like shape that gained more detail before our eyes. The glossy black liquid gained features, formed hands and feet, and broke into strands of straight black hair that fell over a wide forehead.

The creature seemed to shake itself off, testing each limb before tossing the dark head and lifting a cold black gaze to us. Its lips parted, and two rows of small stained teeth were revealed in a cruel smile.

It was George, the wizard we'd come to see. He clasped his hands before him and slid that blustery black gaze over each and every one of us, lingering on Sadie as her tiny body flared with yellow light.

I recognized that light. The small dragon had taken on a storm monster the last time we'd been in the void, single-handedly dispersing its killing tornadoes with her innocent-looking yellow light.

The dragon hadn't come just for show.

"Naida keeper and her wacky crew of misfits and idiots," George said with laughter in his voice. "What a surprise. Did you fall into my path by accident? Or have you lost your collective minds and come looking for me?"

"Hey, George," I said. "How are things in paradise?"

He laughed heartily, each movement leaving behind a swirl of oily black energy. "I'd forgotten how entertaining you could be," he said. Cocking his head, the wizard took another step toward us and then seemed to hit an invisible barrier of some kind.

The wizard stiffened, his smile sliding away. He lifted his hands and slammed his palms against the barrier, a roar rolling across the land. A fresh burst of lava boiled from the top of the volcano and rushed down the mountainside, splashing violently at the bottom.

I glanced around my group, my brows lifted in silent question.

The looks I got back were a mix of confusion and innocence.

Who'd created the barrier?

Slowly, we lifted our gazes to the dragon fluttering on the air above us. Sadie's yellow light had spread a foot in either direction, with tendrils spreading across the distance between the enraged wizard and us.

"Are you doing that?" Sebille quietly asked the amalgamate dragon.

Sadie responded in a chittering tirade that felt like anger.

"What did she say?" I asked the sprite.

"She says he's a bad man who vomits fire."

"She's not wrong," I said.

"What do you want, Keeper?" George asked.

I barely kept from wincing. The next part would be tricky. "I need your help with something."

He slammed a fist on the barrier. "You're not starting off on a good foot."

"We don't trust you, wizard," I told him. "I'm sure you can understand that."

He lifted his hands and flung swirls of black energy at the invisible barrier. I fought the urge to duck as the oily ooze jerked to a halt in mid-air, smeared over the hidden wall, and dripped harmlessly toward the ground.

"We need to ask you about the Pied Piper."

The wizard stilled, his expression turning shrewd. "Ah. I'd heard rumors he was back."

"Tell us what you know about him," Grym demanded.

George narrowed his cold black gaze. "Watch your tone, cop. You can't do anything to me here. I've already been given the stiffest sentence there is." He turned in a circle, arms out, palms up. "Behold my paradise." He flung out a hand and energy slammed into the volcano, exploding the image and sending chunks of black rock and fiery lava into the air.

In a burst of power that made all the hair on my body stand up, Sadie expanded her yellow energy bubble to the size of our group. As it slid over us, cocooning us in its protection, we watched the fiery debris crash down onto us.

In the blink of an eye, George's body was infused with black veining. He started melting into a puddle of acidic black energy.

I'd watched that movie before. I recognized the opening credits. He was about to escape.

Without thinking, I started running.

Rapid, terrified chittering erupted behind me on the hill. Sadie shot past and in front of me, but I ducked beneath her wildly thrashing wings. "Sorry," I yelled. "I need to do this."

George had already started to melt into a puddle of the nasty black acid. He'd dropped eight inches, his feet, ankles, and part of his calves already turned to liquid.

I looked into his ugly face, the thick, black veins turning him from something unattractive to the stuff of nightmares. The horror show was only exacerbated when he smiled. His teeth were small, tight, and though they weren't honed to deadly sharpness like a vampire's, they gave the impression of being just as lethal.

Still, I knew better. It wasn't the wizard's teeth that were lethal.

In a full-out sprint as George melted ever more quickly into his noxious river, I had no time to react when I spotted the slight sheen on the air. My mind barely registered what it meant before I slammed into Sadie's invisible blockade.

Surprise preceded pain, but not for long. A heartbeat later, agony swam through my face and stars burst in front of me. Blood seeped from my nose, and when I reached up to feel the damage, it felt decidedly crooked. "Sadie!"

I hadn't meant my scream to sound like a rebuke, but it came out sounding that way.

The little dragon gave an alarmed chirp and shot skyward, out of reach. Not that I could hurt her even if I wanted to. "Drop the shield, Sadie!" I yelled, shoving to my feet.

George had disappeared up to his armpits and was juicing fast. "Hurry!"

Feet pounded up behind me. I turned to find my crew joining me.

I grabbed Rustin's arm. "Make her drop it. And hurry! He's almost gone."

We all looked at the wizard again. He was up to his shoulders, his eyes gleaming with manic delight. "Until next time, Keeper."

"Rustin!"

Energy swirling around her fists, Sebille burst out into chittering that sounded suspiciously like Sadie's. I'd known Sebille could communicate with and understand the little dragon at a rudimentary level. But what I was hearing was far beyond that.

Sadie shot into the sky, her wings pounding at near hummingbird speed and her movements jerky with fear.

"Do as she says, Sadie," Rustin said in a calm but firm voice.

When she still hesitated, I begged, "Please!" My gaze slid to George again. His manic grin literally melted away, quickly followed by his nose. Only his hate-filled black gaze remained. I figured we had about three seconds before the last few inches of head disappeared, and he was gone.

"Sadie!"

With agonizing slowness, the dragon let the strands of her magic shrink, the fibers thinning with a sluggishness that brought my blood pressure spiking to my ears. I bit back a frustrated scream, not wanting to scare her again and slow it down even further.

But, by the time the magic dissipated slowly and the barrier wall soughed away, only about an inch of George's head still sat above the blistering liquid.

Too late! We were too late.

In desperation, I started to step closer, only to jump back with a screech of pain as the black river shot toward my feet, eating the toes of my sneakers away with diabolical ease.

The river spread outward, pushing us inexorably away with every frustrating second.

Half an inch of George's skull was all that showed by the time Bandy Joe grabbed the lei from my hand.

I whirled on him with an outraged squawk. "What...?"

He held the lei up in front of him, silver energy winding around it to create a solid hoop with the artifact. Perched on his shoulder, Zoom slowly blinked, his bulging orange gaze locked onto the lei.

Joe held up his free hand. "Interdimensional horseshoe champion for five years in a row," he told me. "I've got this."

I nodded, cognizant of our quickly closing window.

We all turned back to the wizard. My stomach

twisted with despair as I saw that only a few strands of his hair still sat atop the oozing energy.

Joe took a deep breath, assumed the horseshoe tossing stance, and let fly.

Like transfixed observers at the aforementioned interdimensional horseshoe competition, we all watched as the lei spun through the air, aimed like an arrow at its target, and plopped into the ooze just as the last of George's hairs was sucked down into the magical excretion.

We stood in disappointed silence as the lei followed George into the goo, finally disappearing from sight.

"Buzzard boogers!" I screamed, beyond frustrated. The scream earned me another worried chirp from Sadie.

"Okay," Grym said, ever practical. "We need a Plan B."

Sebille frowned. "We might want to have this discussion somewhere else," she said, pointing at the black acid flowing our way.

We all took three giant steps back, eyeing it.

I shook my head at Grym. "We're not going to get another chance at him. He knows we're looking for him now."

"Guys," Rustin said.

"We know where to find him," Bandy Joe said. "He can't really hide from us."

I swung my arms around the vast, blank canvas

of the void. "Are you serious? Look around you. Anything goes in this place. It's only limited by his imagination."

"Well, there you go," Grym said. "He's just a wizard. How much imagination could he have?"

Despite my bone-deep frustration, I snorted out a laugh.

"Um, Naida," Rustin said again.

Sebille walked over to Rustin and Sadie dropped to her shoulder, chittering rapidly in her ear.

"Something's happening here," Rustin said.

We finally stopped arguing long enough to look at the shifter witch. He pointed toward the puddle of black energy. We followed his gaze, and I blinked. The puddle had stopped spreading. That was good. But, more interestingly, the center of the puddle was bulging upward. As it continued to grow and stretch, I realized...

I grabbed Grym's arm. "He's coming back."

11

YEAH, YEAH. STOP TALKING

George rose up from the muck with a growl. "I'll kill you all!" he roared as soon as his mouth and chest were back.

Sebille rolled her eyes. "Yeah, yeah. Stop talking."

We all blinked in surprise. Apparently, Sebille was back to fighting form. I wondered if she'd gotten her magical mojo back. She moved forward, eyeing the lei artifact, which looked as good as new and smelled even better. "We just need some information, and then we'll take that thing off and you can go on your way."

His entire body back to its normal, unpleasant form, George's gaze rolled toward the lei around his neck, and a cunning smile crossed his face. He jerked as if stung by a wasp and frowned. He jerked again. And again. Each time looking more confused.

I finally realized what he was doing. "You can't use your magic until we take it off. The faster you give us what we need, the faster you'll be free."

"Free?" he ground out on a growl. "You call this free?"

I shrugged. Dropping him into the void had been an accident. I hadn't known what that gun artifact would do when I'd fired it at him. In my defense, I'd been under a lot of pressure at the time, seeing as he'd been trying to kill all my friends and me. "If you're willing to be judged for your behavior, we can see about bringing you back."

That got his attention. "What behavior?"

"You called me an explosion of paint shaped like a girl," Sebille said, glowering at him.

For a moment, he looked like he couldn't believe what he was hearing. Then he burst into laughter.

Much to the sprite's chagrin, we all joined him.

When she painted us with a glare, I said, "You have to admit, that was funny."

Sebille huffed out a disgusted breath.

"You and your friend attacked us twice," I told George. "You need to answer for that."

He thought about it for a beat and then nodded. "Agreed."

Finally, we were getting somewhere.

"Okay." I looked at Bandy Joe.

He stepped forward. "Wizard, I am Bandy Joe Barrows, a KoA from Earth's mirror dimension."

I blinked in surprise. I hadn't known his dimension was Earth's mirror dimension. Though, if I thought about it, that made sense. His dimension was the only one I knew of that had an identical town called Enchanted, right down to a Croakies and the herbal store next door run by the mirror version of Lea.

"I hold the piper's original pipe in my toxic magic vault."

George suddenly found the spongy black horizon more interesting than Bandy Joe. Guilt painted lines over every muscle and feature.

"Endeara of the enchanted woods sent us to you. She believes you have the ability to create coercive artifacts. Is this true?"

George's wandering gaze finally settled on Joe. He seemed reluctant to answer. The wizard skimmed a look at me, and I could almost read the thoughts sliding through his sick mind. He wanted out of the void. He just had to decide how much he wanted it.

"It's probably kind of hard to do business here in the abyss, isn't it?" I prodded.

"If I help you find that artifact, you need to promise to get me out of here."

"We'll agree to take you back in police custody," Grym said. "You'll get your day in court. There are no guarantees as to the results."

George's shoulders jerked in an awkward shrug.

"Even the Casa De Grimoire would be better than this place."

Casa De Grimoire was the cute little name the darker side of the magical population had for the Société's prison system.

"You admit you made the compelling pipe?" Sebille asked.

"I did."

"Did you insert a tracking device inside?" I asked.

The wizard's grin was mean. "The client requested I not insert such a device."

Fighting frustration, I had to wonder why the man looked so happy. If he believed we'd take him out of the void without getting the pipe's location, he was sadly mistaken.

"But you inserted one anyway, didn't you?" Rustin asked, stepping forward.

George's smile widened. "I couldn't insert a device, no."

Losing patience, I threw up my hands. He clearly had more to say, but he was being a baboon's butt about it. "Okay, well, I guess we'll be on our way then," I said. "Have a nice life."

"Not so fast," the wizard barked out.

"Stop playing us for fools!" Sebille said. "Tell us whether you can track the pipe or not."

George sighed, disgusted that we were cutting his little game short. "I didn't insert a device. But I did coat the item with a tracking spell. My reputation is linked to every artifact I create. I never let one go out the door without knowing I can find it if I have to." He narrowed his eyes on me. "And if you ever tell anybody that, I'll deny it and call you a liar."

"I have no desire to get in the way of your little scheme," I told him. Prison would do that quite nicely. "We need you to find the artifact for us."

He grinned again. The sight made me distinctly uncomfortable. "Absolutely. I'll just need you to remove this entrapment artifact and take me back with you."

I shook my head. "That's not the deal."

"Ah, but it is the deal, Naida keeper. You see, if you want me to locate that pipe, I'll need access to my home in the earthly dimension."

Grym shook his head. "Tell us where the tracker is. Once we've found the pipe, we'll get you out of here."

"That won't work for me," George insisted.

"Too bad," Grym said.

George sighed again. Apparently, we were being very challenging. "Believe it or not, I'm not trying to be difficult, Detective Grym. Not at this moment. Though, I'll look for every opportunity in the future to do so. I'm just telling you the way it is. What you're looking for is not something that you can just walk in and pick up. It's etched into the very fabric of my home. And it needs my magic signature to engage it."

Wizard George lived in a nondescript apartment building on the south side of Enchanted. It was a fairly rough area with a questionable element in the form of street gangs. George had been part of the biggest street gang when we'd had our altercation that had ended with him swimming in the abyss. We'd bumped up against him and one of his weasly sidekicks when we'd come to the apartment building to relieve an unfortunate resident of the Groundhog Day alarm clock that had rocked his world in a decidedly bad way.

George and the aforementioned sidekick had been smoking on the stoop that night, and he'd forced us to go through him to get to our rogue artifact.

It hadn't worked out well for George.

Grym and Rustin flanked George, who walked stiffly under the influence of the lei restraint.

Sebille and Bandy Joe, with Zoom, stood next to me as we watched the three men heading our way from Grym's car. We'd stopped by Croakies on the way so I could grab Slimy and my own car.

"I might need to borrow that lei for my next date," Sebille said in a thoughtful voice.

I blinked in surprise. "Date? Since when do you date?"

She rolled her eyes so hard I could hear her skull creak.

"He's very powerful," Joe said as Zoom and Slimy made bulgy eyes at each other.

"Huh?" I responded in a typical example of my razor-sharp wit.

"Your frog, Mr. Slimy." Joe grimaced at the name, clearly not a fan.

"Oh. Yeah. I mean, he is?"

Joe nodded. "But his aura is funny. It's fractured."

"Long story. Suffice it to say he didn't start out that way in life." I looked down at the frog nestled safely inside my cupped palms. "I'll need your input on the magic when we get inside."

There's something going on up there, Slimy responded. *On the roof.*

Joe blinked in surprise. "I'll do my best. But reading signatures isn't really my strong suit."

I realized he'd thought I was talking to him. I shook my head. "I was actually talking to Slimy."

Joe's eyes went wide. "You can communicate with him? Verbally?"

"Yes. I mean, he doesn't talk exactly. I can hear him in my head."

"Fascinating." Joe narrowed his gaze on my frog and then slid the assessing glance toward Zoom. His expression turned constipated.

I twisted my lips to hide a grin as Zoom blinked blankly back at him.

"Where are we going?" Rustin asked as they stopped in front of us.

George jerked his head upward. "I'm on the roof."

Slimy had been right. "Nicely done, frog. Slap me five, or in your case, four." He tapped my palm with his little webbed foot. *You may call me Prince.*

I snorted out a laugh. We followed the men into the building and hit the stairs because, apparently, the elevator didn't go all the way to the roof. "What kind of apartment is this, anyway?" I asked the wizard.

He sliced me with a sharp glance. "It's *my* kind of apartment."

Rustin pushed the door open and held it as Grym guided George through with a grip on his arm.

I stepped onto the stone and tar roof and looked around, my eyes going round. Sebille stepped up beside me, her lean muscles stiffening in shock. "Holy mother of all goddesses. What has this guy been doing up here?"

The entire center of the roof was burned into a pentagram. Each point of the symbol was fitted with thick black pillar candles in varying heights. The length of their use showed in the drips and puddles of dried wax beneath them. Positioned at the very center of the enormous symbol was a skull. Inside the jaw was another candle, which was white and much smaller than the pillars at the points. Something that looked like blood spilled over the skull and stained the candle inside.

"Why does that look like a human skull?" Grym growled. His aura shifted and writhed around him, and I was afraid he was going to burst into his gargoyle form if I didn't do something fast. "Grym. Let him explain. Maybe it's not what it looks like."

But George was either oblivious or very stupid. "Yep. It's human."

A button popped off Grym's shirt as his body started to swell.

I hurried over and laid a hand on his arm. "Remember the stakes here. Let's hear him out."

Though a low growl throbbed in Grym's wide chest, he held himself together as we all looked at George.

The wizard played coy. "What?"

"Where did you get a human skull?" I asked very slowly as if talking to a mentally challenged goblin. Well, that was actually a bit redundant.

"Oh. You think I killed someone for their skull?" He laughed, and the growl in Grym's chest deepened. I tightened my grip on his arm.

Okay, that was it. I was so over wizards. "Wizard, stop being stupid. You're about to have three hundred pounds of gargoyle all up in your grill. Explain quickly and carefully how that human skull got there and, don't forget the part about all that blood."

"It's the skull of a dead wizard. He died of natural causes." He grimaced. "Well, if you can call being eaten by an angry demon natural."

I peaked my brows. "Demon?"

"Long story. Very boring..."

I highly doubted that.

"But, I didn't kill him. He was very powerful. His residual magic is more than many live wizards I know. He's my magic engine."

Grym's prodigious musculature softened, and he shrank back to normal size. But the distaste coloring his expression when he looked upon George never wavered. I realized my boyfriend was really going to enjoy putting the wizard behind bars.

"Okay, let's get to it," Sebille said, cutting right through all the extraneous stuff like anger and other emotions as if they were little more than bad-smelling air.

Her lack of compassion was showing again.

George rolled his eyes downward. "I need this thing off."

"Not a chance," Rustin said.

"Then I can't do anything. I need to be able to use my magic."

Grym and I shared a look. I gave him the tiniest of nods. "We need to do this," I whispered. "There's more riding on it than you know."

He held my gaze for a long moment and then nodded, trusting me.

That trust made warmth blossom in my belly. I wasn't used to someone trusting my instincts like that. It was a side effect of being kind of a screwup. And, on the heels of that thought, I prayed I wasn't screwing up by letting the wizard free.

Grym looked at Bandy Joe and nodded. As the one who'd locked George into the lei's magic, he had to be the one to release him.

Bandy Joe stepped close to the wizard and reached for the lei around his neck. He hesitated for the briefest time, his frog-like black gaze locked on George's. For just a beat, Joe's squat form tensed, and panic did a quick, painful slice through my middle.

Was I wrong to release him? I knew he couldn't be trusted. He'd have nothing to lose by attacking us and taking off. On the other hand, if he did as we asked, he was going to prison.

The panic turned feral, digging deep gouges out of my guts and making it hard to breathe.

I opened my mouth to stop the other keeper, but it was too late.

With a quick flick of his wrists, Joe tugged the lei over George's head, and the wizard was free.

George smiled. The sight of that smile sucked all the air out of the space where we stood.

12

YOU ARE AWARE THAT HE'S PULLING A
SHLOAD OF POWER, RIGHT?

B lack veining rose upward from the vee of George's shirt, thickening and bulging beneath his skin even as I watched in horror. The veins trailed down his arms, visibly pulsing as they stretched into his hands, turning his long fingers black.

Slimy gave a nervous little hop on my hand and liquid trickled into my palm.

Oops! Sorry, he yelped. *I don't like this, Naida*

The fact that I didn't even react to his peeing on me was proof of how discombobulated I was by the wizard's antics.

"Naida?" Grym asked, his body swelling toward his gargoyle form just in case.

Bandy Joe's gaze shot to me and widened, making him look even more like his favorite reptile than usual. He lifted the lei. "Should I put this back on him?"

I stared into the wizard's black eyes, seeing the twinkle of amusement in their icy depths. The panic that had started to rise slowed, and the tightening in my chest loosened. I arched a brow at George.

He laughed. "I'm not pulling a fast one, Naida keeper. I'm just doing as you asked."

Biting the inside of my lip with uncertainty, I stretched out a hand to stop Grym and Joe. "Let's see what he's up to." I comforted myself with the knowledge that George would need time to melt all the way down. We could easily trap him again if that happened.

Black energy flowed from his fingertips and dripped downward, hitting the pentagram with a sizzle and sliding through the grooves of the symbol, filling it. When the entire symbol was full of George's midnight-colored magic, the candles at each point burst into flame. The fire rose a foot into the air and then settled back to normal height.

The last candle to flame up was the one inside the skull. As soon as the fire flashed into existence, the thing started to tremble, the bones clanking against the roof's surface with an almost meaty sound that was beyond disturbing.

Then a charcoal fog began to sift upward from beneath the skull, lifting it off the ground until it was at the wizard's eye level. It hung there, the eye sockets glowing an eerie shade of red as the candle flame filled the entire skull with fire.

George's eyes started to glow red too.

I must have made a sound of disgust because Sebille caught my eye, her green gaze widening in sympathy.

You are aware that he's pulling a shload of power, right? Slimy asked. He sounded as worried as I felt.

"It'll be all right," I told him. "We need to let him do his thing."

"Are you trying to convince yourself or me?" Grym responded. I didn't bother telling him I'd been talking to the frog. The message worked for him too. I really didn't think we had a choice.

"Just in case," Rustin said. "I think we should spread out around the pentagram. We'd have a better chance of stopping him."

I nodded. "Good idea."

We spread out equidistant to each other around the enormous, ugly star.

Almost immediately, energy began to roil around Sebille, Rustin, and Joe's fingertips. Grym had no magic to call, but I noticed he'd slipped off his shoes and removed his shirt in preparation for a quick change to his gargoyle form.

Something's happening, Slimy warned me.

Nothing appeared to have changed from my perspective. But the frog had mad magic reading abilities, and he hadn't been wrong yet. "Look alive," I told everyone.

The candle flames suddenly shot to the height of the skull and stayed there, the flames flaring into a rainbow of colors, from yellow to orange to green to blue. The color switches danced to an unknown rhythm, each candle seemingly playing a different tune. Then, in a move that was sure to give me night-mares for the rest of my life, the jaws of the skull opened with an audible creak, and a deep, rusty voice emerged from between them. The language it spoke was indecipherable, at least by me, but it had a guttural tone that made me think of demonic speech. I recog-nized only one small part of whatever it said. A series of numbers and letters that meant nothing to me.

I jumped as the candle flames exploded upward again, emitting a high-pitched wheezing noise that sent the skull spinning faster and faster until its terrifying features were nothing more than a blur.

Then, just as suddenly as it started, the candle flames plunged downward and extinguished, and the skull dropped to the roof with a thud.

George stood there a moment longer, his eyes still aglow.

We watched him carefully, still ready for trouble. But the oily black energy retraced its path back to George. Within minutes, the veining in his body had shrunk and disappeared. Finally, he turned a cognizant black gaze to me. "The pipe you seek is in the demonic dimension, at the following coordinates." He rambled off a long series of numbers while I flinched. I'd forget them the minute I heard them. I opened my mouth to ask him to repeat the coordinates, but he sagged downward, falling to the ground in an unconscious heap.

I looked around the circle. "Did anybody get those?"

Joe and Rustin flinched.

"I got the first part," Rustin said. "But it was too fast."

"I got some of the middle," Sebille said.

Grym pulled his shirt back over his head. "He lost me at demonic dimension."

Sebille snorted out a laugh.

I sighed. "I think I might be able to remember the last part. We'll just have to try to piece together what we each heard."

daeLat: 40 degrees, 42 minutes, 51 seconds N, daeLong: 74 degrees, 0 minutes, 21 seconds W, Slimy blurted. *Which is actually the same coordinates as New York City except in the demonic realm.*

I stared at the fat squish. He twitched and blinked, his throat working faster than usual under the scrutiny. *What?* he finally asked.

"What are you, some kind of idiot savant with coordinates?"

He twitched again in what I was pretty sure had been a froggy shrug.

I repeated what he'd said as best I could remember.

"So you're saying we're going to demonic New York City?" Grym asked.

I nodded. "Let's get the wizard to jail. Then..."

We all turned toward where George had landed and blinked.

Blithering bat bunions.

George was in the wind.

I couldn't sleep. I'd barely been able to eat, which was something. Nothing short of imminent death usually turned me off my feed.

But knowing we were down one day already in our three-day timeline was enough to do it. I kept thinking I should get out of bed and head to the demonic realm.

Then I'd think about bumping up against demons in the middle of the night, and I'd rethink the idea. Then, I'd wonder if the demonic realm was in the same timeline as we were. For all I knew, it could be morning there.

What if it *was* morning there? That would mean that if we waited for what was a decent hour for us, we'd be walking into demonic New York in the middle of the night.

And, having gone full circle, I was off again.

I finally climbed out of bed, more exhausted than when I went into it. I headed into the kitchen, intending to fix myself a cup of Chamomile tea to help me sleep. I turned on the faucet to fill the teapot, and nothing happened.

Frowning, I turned it off and then back on again.

Nothing.

In a fit of creative desperation, I sang the magic muffin song, hoping that might unstop it.

The toilet in my bathroom flushed. The water still didn't come out of the faucet.

Le sigh...

I slipped my feet into slippers and headed downstairs. Behind me, a soft thump announced that Wicked was coming with me. Fenwald stretched and sighed, not even tempted to rouse himself.

When I got to the bottom of the steps, I looked around, hoping to see Baca, our new resident brownie, so I could ask her to fix the faucet. I didn't see her, but I did hear Bandy Joe snoring from his cot in the library.

I followed the soft murmur of voices in the bookstore. The sound alarmed me at first, until I realized who it had to be.

Hobs was sitting on top of the first in a row of near-ceiling-height bookshelves, spindly legs dangling and equally skinny arms flailing the air as he told a story to the pretty little brownie clinging to the side of the same bookshelf. Baca was making use of a small drill that looked like a toy but sounded real.

Hobs stopped mid-sentence, his head whipping in my direction. Baca's expression told me she was about to bolt. She'd lived at Croakies for several weeks, but the brownie still wasn't accustomed to Sebille or me. Though, she was much better than she used to be. At least she didn't pop away with a yelp whenever we came across her anymore.

I held up a hand, giving her what I hoped was a soothing smile. "It's okay. Please stay."

Baca glanced at Hobs and then nodded. "Yes, Miss." The brownie had picked up on Hobs's way of addressing me, though I'd tried to break her of it. She'd proved to be just as intractable as the little hobgoblin on the issue.

"I guess this is why I haven't seen you around much during the day lately," I told Hobs.

He shrugged. "Baca likes the company." Then he seemed to rethink my comment, and I could see the moment when he had the thought he'd made me unhappy. "I'm sorry, Miss. I can get up earlier if you want."

"No. You're fine. I'm glad you two have a chance to visit."

He nodded.

A sad feeling came over me when I looked at the little guy. Hobs seemed to have matured over the months he'd lived with us. He hardly ever asked Sebille to beat him up anymore. I couldn't remember the last time he'd slid down the banister in the artifact library to smack against the wall. Ever since he'd been so badly poisoned by the evil Cupid queen, he'd been quieter and more subdued.

Or maybe it was because of Baca's arrival. As I had the thought, I became aware of a tiny niggle of resentment for the little brownie. I immediately felt guilty about it. She didn't deserve my resentment. She'd done everything she could to make herself useful.

"Baca, there's something wrong with my faucet upstairs. Do you think you can take a look at it?"

She gave the drill one final whirl and then jumped nimbly from the shelf, landing lightly on her tiny feet. Hobs jumped down next to her.

They looked so cute together. Though he was only a little over two feet tall himself, Hobs was a few inches taller than the brownie, and he was pale to her warm brown skin tone. He had a shock of light brown hair between two big ears, big blue eyes, a shortish body, and long legs and arms with spidery fingers. He was dressed in his usual white tunic and plain white pants.

Becca was like a fairy, with mahogany brown hair that fell past her shoulders, warm brown eyes, and perfectly proportioned limbs. She wore a pale brown tunic over tan leggings and had a crown of flowers around her silky hair. As usual, a plain, brown leather tool belt encircled her waist, the handles of a variety of household tools sticking up from the pockets.

I was a little surprised she didn't immediately run upstairs. She generally got very excited about having a new repair to do. "I don't need to go up, Miss. I turned the water off so I could fix the leak in the downstairs bathroom sink."

"Ah," I said. It would be nice to get that leak fixed. The constant drip, drip, drip was annoying throughout my workday, and it was leaving an unpleasant rust residue behind. "Okay, I won't worry about it then."

"I can do that now," she offered shyly, the thick fringe of lashes falling over her eyes.

"It's not a big deal. I was just going to make some tea."

Baca nodded. "I can make tea, Miss." She flashed away so quickly she was a blur on the air. I watched her turn the heat up under a tea pot she must have filled before she turned off the water. Always thinking, that brownie.

I glanced at Hobs. "I don't suppose you know anything about the demonic realm?"

I'd really just been making conversation, my mind too tired to form an actual thought beyond the cup of tea Baca was making. The little brownie was good at most things she tried. But she excelled at two things. She could repair anything non-physiological like nobody's business. And she made a cup of tea that even rivaled Sebille's for tastiness. Where the sprite was inarguably tea-talented, Baca was tea-ceptional.

Hobs's little face paled, no easy feat since he was already as pale as milk. "You're going into the demonic realm, Miss?"

I nodded, trying to appear more confident than I was. "We're going to retrieve the rogue pipe artifact from the piper."

His little face puckered into an unhappy frown. "It's very dangerous there, Miss."

Baca handed me a steaming cuppa and I thanked her, inhaling its aromatic steam with a sigh. "I know. But it can't be helped. Having the Pied Piper running around Enchanted hurting..." I swallowed hard, thinking of the elderly ogre woman lying on the table. "...and killing can't be allowed. It's my job to wrangle the artifact."

"Doesn't the demonic realm have its own Keeper of the Artifacts?" he asked.

My head shot up as his words made something snick into place in my brain. Of course. That was what had been niggling at me. "I suppose it does." I realized I would have to touch base with that KoA. There really weren't any rules about checking in when we worked in another KoA's territory. But it seemed wise.

I sighed. One more task to be added to the list. I made a mental note to ask Rustin to contact his aunt Madeline in the morning. She'd know who the other KoA was and how I could contact him or her.

"They might want to handle it themselves," Hobs said. I realized he'd been speaking while my mind wandered through details.

I shook my head. "The piper is hurting people here, in my realm. I have jurisdiction." I really didn't know if Keepers even used such legal terms to delineate boundaries of responsibility. I liked to think in those terms because I was a fan of police and forensic science TV.

Hobs sat in silence for a long moment, drawing my gaze to him. "What?"

He blinked his large blue eyes, his oversized ears twitching as he frowned. "I'm going with you."

I opened my mouth to argue, but Hobs cut me off with a raised hand. "I lived there, Miss. I can help."

I thought about it for a long moment and then nodded. "Okay. That's a good idea. We can use someone who knows the lay of the land. Thanks, Hobs."

A soft sound worked its way into my consciousness. I frowned as I realized it was a drill. I looked toward the kitchen and frowned. "Where's Baca?"

Hobs frowned too, three shallow horizontal lines creasing his forehead. "I don't know, Miss. Maybe she went upstairs to fix your..." Hobs's skinny arms flew up, and he yelped as the chair beneath his butt jolted. One leg fell out from underneath him, sending the chair crashing backward and him slamming to the floor on a grunt of pain.

I jumped to my feet, my gaze flying around the room looking for our attacker.

Soft giggling sounded from somewhere behind the massive bookshelves.

I looked down at Hobs. He blinked a couple of times slowly, and then a wide grin spread across his face. His arms flew into the air and he yelled, "Again!"

The giggling in the shadows turned to belly laughs.

I shook my head, hiding a smile. Apparently, the little guy hadn't grown up *that* much after all.

13

HE THINKS FLIES ARE BETTER THAN CRICKETS. CLEARLY, HE'S AN IDIOT

We couldn't use the Book of Pages to travel inter-dimensionally, so we needed to use the broken communicating mirror again. Unfortunately, we had three times the number of people as the last time, when we'd traveled to Bandy's Joe's dimension.

We stood in front of the mirror and stared into the fractured glass of the mirror, our expressions contemplative.

"Maybe Zoom and I can send you two at a time and come through last," Joe suggested.

I knew that would be hard on the little frog and said so, earning myself a look of respect from Joe and a nod.

"Do you have a communicating mirror in your dimension?" Grym asked Joe.

"I do."

"We could split up and use his mirror too," Grym suggested.

"Same problem," I said. My brows lifted. "That would require two dimensional hops instead of one. Unless..."

Ribbit! sayeth the fat squish down by my feet. We all looked down at Mr. Slimy. He blinked up at me. *I can up my wattage,* he told me. *The little tree frog and I both can.*

His name is Zoom, I told the squish.

Slimy shrugged. *He's kind of a dummy, but he has a lot of power. And so do I.*

A dummy? Why would you say that? He seems very nice.

He thinks flies are better than crickets. Clearly, he's an idiot.

I think egg rolls are better than any bug. Does that make me stupid too?

Slimy snorted out a laugh in my mind. *I can't believe you had to ask. That's a given.*

I glared down at him.

"Um, Naida?" Grym asked. "What's happening?"

I gave a guilty jolt. "Oh. Sorry. I was talking to the green bus." I called him that because he'd been Rustin's only transportation for the first several months I'd known him. When he'd still been the ghost witch. Unfortunately, or fortunately, depending on your perspective, the frog came out of the experience of having a disembodied witch sharing his skin with advanced thought processes and a ton of attitude. "He says he can help."

Rustin cleared his throat. "Naida?"

I glanced his way.

"I'm not going with you on this trip," he told me.

"You're not? Why?"

"Somebody needs to keep an eye on things here. Since I'm not much good to you unless you want me to break out the chimera..."

Oh goddess, no! Not that! I didn't say the words out loud, but the sentiment must have shown on my face.

He gave me a grim smile. "Yeah. It's probably best not to bring him out in the demonic dimension. They'll see it as a sign of aggression and get testy."

"I'm staying here too," Sebille said. "I'll keep Wicked. New Baal is no place for a cat. Demons don't like cats. When they see a cat, they have a tendency to attack first and ask no questions at all."

"Are you sure you don't want to come?" Sebille never backed down from a challenge. Maybe I needed to plan an intervention for her. "You know how much is at stake with this."

Anger filled her bright green gaze. She stiffened with affront. "Of course I do, Naida. That's why I'm staying here. There's something I need to do. It's related to this issue. I think it's just as important."

We stared at each other for a long moment. Her expression told me she wasn't going to change her mind, and mine was aimed at trying to make sure she wasn't just giving up. Finally, I nodded. There was a flicker of fire in her eye that made me feel better. "Okay. Keep me posted?"

She nodded, her bony shoulders relaxing.

I grabbed Hobs's hand and glanced at Grym and Bandy Joe. "I guess it's just us then." Sending energy into the mirror, I grimaced at the heaviness suddenly pressing into me. A moment later, I yelped softly as invisible hands grabbed hold of my shoulders and ripped us into the mirror.

We stomped down onto concrete, a couple of us stumbling forward with loud, clumsy steps.

Okay, that might have just been me. But, hey, at least I didn't slide across the concrete on my face. I was getting better.

Hobs's hand ripped from mine and he flew away, the squish clutched inside a cage of his long fingers. He slammed into a brick wall at the side of the alley where we'd landed, hanging on the rough brick like a smushed fly against a window, and then crumpled slowly downward, laughing hysterically.

Bandy Joe stared at him in horror for a long moment and then slid his disbelieving gaze toward me.

I shrugged. "I have no words."

Grym stood at the mouth of the alley, looking out

over the city, which we'd learned from researching it before we left, was called New Baal rather than New York. I walked up beside him and bumped his shoulder with my own. "Hey. How does it look?"

He gave me a glance that made my innards heat and pointed toward a very odd skyline in the distance. All of the buildings were pointed at the top, like spears. "The city has very aggressive architecture. From where we're standing it looks a lot like one of our cities."

"But not like New York," I murmured. I'd only visited New York a couple of times, but I'd seen pictures of it lots of times.

"No. Not like New York."

"According to this map," Bandy Joe said, "...it looks like the KoA is just down this street a few blocks."

I peered down the line of spare, unimaginative buildings running the length of the street on both sides and noted the lack of signs sticking out from the structures. I stepped onto a surprisingly well-kept sidewalk and looked at the front of the closest buildings, seeing nothing but a few scribbles in black paint beside each door. "No signs." The odd symbols painted on the brick and stone reminded me of Chinese characters, except they were more linear. The individual characters were more rounded, like cursive English, but they flowed together rather than standing at attention next to each other like the form of writing I was used to. The most important difference was that, like the architecture, their written language seemed steeped in violence. Symbols that looked like bloody daggers stabbed into figures that seemed to explode from the surface they were drawn on. One symbol looked like a noose. Another like a spear. I recognized one symbol as a pentacle, and many of the "words" if that was what they were, were topped with what could only be called horns.

Grym frowned. "Do either of you read demonish?"

Joe and I both shook our heads.

"I do," said Mr. Giggles in his high-pitched voice. Hobs turned and pointed to a building well down the street, which was built of some kind of red brick that sparked different colors in the sunlight. "It's down there."

"Are you sure?" I asked.

His response was to start skipping down the sidewalk, his manner as carefree as a day in Enchanted Park.

Somehow, looking at those aggressive buildings and violent symbols, I doubted our little outing would be that benign.

Next to the symbols on the red building, on a rough-looking piece of paper with big pieces of visible wood in its weave, someone had painted a stylized KoA in bright green paint. The note had been attached to the door with a large knife, making it look like a threat rather than information.

Looking at that knife, which seemed to have something brown and crusty in the seam where the handle met the blade, I wondered if we might not be better off just trying to find the piper on our own.

Just as I was about to turn on my heel and run like the sissy girl I was, the door flew open, nearly smacking me in the face. A hand snaked through the opening and grabbed the knife. The huge, clawed hand pulled the knife out of the petrified wood of the door as if it were butter and then retracted back into the building before closing the door in our faces.

"Hm," said Bandy Joe. "Their exterior doors open outwardly here. Fascinating."

I gave him a bland look. "Is it?"

"It is, actually," Grym agreed.

"Because nothing else about what just happened is pertinent," I mumbled, my tone wry.

They squinted at me as if they suspected I was being ironic but weren't quite sure. I huffed. "We might as well get this over with." Yes, I realize I'd been ready to tuck tail and skedaddle a moment earlier. But if the KoA was that scary, what did that say about the rest of the population in Baal? The devil, pun intended, we knew was slightly better than the devil we didn't.

I pulled the door open and, taking a deep breath, stepped inside and jolted to a stop.

Sitting behind a pile of wooden crates that was apparently supposed to serve as a desk was something...someone...something I couldn't identify. Except to note that it was clutching the knife from the door in a meaty clawed fist and seemed to be brandishing it at a small creature with black eyes and green fur that was standing over a puddle which I assumed shouldn't be there. The poor thing looked absolutely terrified, and it was panting as its eyes bulged with fear. As we came into the room, the little furry thing turned our way and gave its ragged tail a hopeful wag.

Yeah. That wasn't good.

I frowned at the horned creature with the knife. "What's going on here?"

I felt Grym come up beside me, his big body edging forward as if he would throw himself at the creature if it came for me.

The horned creature straightened slowly from its chair, rising...and rising...and rising...

I gulped. That sucker was tall!

He had a wide face with a flat nose and nostrils that flared as if he was scenting us to take our measure. Something moved along the floor behind him. I blinked as a wide, meaty snake slithered around the creature's feet.

I opened my mouth to tell him about the reptile

but forgot what I was about to say when he slammed the blade into the makeshift desk, making the whole rickety structure tremble.

There was a whir of movement. I was suddenly holding Slimy, and the little furry creature was missing from the desk. I turned around and found the doglike creature clutched protectively in Hobs's spindly arms. Hobs was inches from the door, clearly ready to bolt.

The creature behind the desk narrowed its scary red eyes at Hobs. I stepped forward. "You won't touch him or any of my people."

I was shocked to hear myself speak. There hadn't even been a quiver in my voice.

"And who are you?" The thing's voice was sibilant, snakelike. The meaty reptile beneath the desk unraveled itself and straightened, following the creature out from behind the desk. That was when I realized it wasn't a snake. It was a really long tail with a hissing snake's head at its tip.

Sweet Caroline in a canoe.

"I don't like to repeat myself," the creature hissed.

Forcing my spine to straighten, I lifted my chin. If I was going to die in New Baal, I'd go out with dignity. "I'm Naida Griffith, Keeper of the Artifacts for the Earthly dimension. Who are you?"

He sneered at me, showing a lot of really scary teeth. "Did you not read the sign out front?"

I felt my eyes go wide. "You're the Keeper?"

He lifted his brows, or really his brow bones. He didn't seem to have any hair on his leathery body. "If this is the Keeper's office, why would I be here if I wasn't the Keeper?"

I glanced at Bandy Joe. He widened his eyes in silent commiseration. I'd met a few other Keepers since becoming one myself. Each had been unique. Some had been unpleasant. But the guy standing in front of us was beyond understanding.

"What were you going to do to that creature?" Grym asked.

The horned one skimmed his attention to the detective. "And who are you?"

"Detective Wise Grym from the Enchanted Police. Can we have your name?"

The creature smiled. "Not unless you're ready to die."

Alrighty then.

We all blinked at him for a minute, and then he started to laugh. A full-on belly laugh that made his tail flop around behind him. "I love that one. Non-demons always pee themselves when I break that one out."

Grym didn't look amused. "We'd like to know who we're dealing with."

Mr. Horns nodded. "I'm sure you would. But you're not getting my name. Historically, it hasn't worked out well for demons who gave their names out like candy."

"So what should we call you?" Joe asked.

The horned one shrugged, unconcerned by our dilemma. "I'd like it best if you didn't call me at all." He reached into the mess of crates and fumbled around for a minute before coming up with a roll of paper. He stabbed it toward me. "Your PTB called and told me you were coming. This map will help you find the piper. What you do with him from that point on is between you and the Magical Universe." He flapped his clawed hand toward the door. "Don't let the backdraft blow your skirts up." He jerked his chin toward the little green creature. "Leave that behind when you go."

I narrowed my gaze on him. "Is that your pet?"

Mr. Horns glared back at me. "Not your business."

"It is if you plan to mistreat it."

Watch out, said the frog. *He's cooking something up.*

A thick wash of silver-gray magic rose from the KoA like an aura, throbbing with barely suppressed aggression. "Leave now, and I won't kill you all."

Trickle, trickle.

"Ah!" I exclaimed, grimacing down at the frog pee on my palm.

Sorry! This guy's seriously upping the terror factor.

I didn't think the devilish KoA could really hurt us. Not with his Keeper magic anyway. If it was like mine, it was really only good for curling hair or inducing its victims to pee themselves.

I frowned down at my wet palm. Apparently it worked.

Realizing the creature with the hissing tail had other weapons at his disposal—built-in weapons—I inclined my head and turned away. Joe was right behind me, but Grym held back. I stopped at the door and glanced at him. "Grym?"

"Go on out, Naida. I'll be right there."

He joined us on the sidewalk a few minutes later, his color high and his jaw tight. "Let's go."

"What about that?" Bandy Joe asked, sliding a skeptical eye over the little green creature.

Hobs's arms tightened around it, causing the pitiful little thing to whimper softly. "We can't let her go back there, Miss," Hobs said, his tone militant.

I totally agreed. "You're right. We can't. But I don't want you to get your hopes up, Hobs," I warned. "We can't keep it."

"She's a her, Miss," Hobs said, beaming at me like he hadn't even heard what I'd said.

Grym nudged us into movement. "Do you have that map?" he asked me.

I pulled it out of the backpack purse I was wearing and bobbled it, sending it toward the side-walk. "Oh, sorry." My nerves were all atwitch. The way Grym kept looking back over his shoulder was making me jumpy. "Is he coming after us?"

Grym snatched the map before it hit the ground and unrolled it. "Not if he wants to hold onto his Keeper license."

Bandy Joe's eyes went wide. "You can get his license taken away?"

Grym was busy eyeing the map. He glanced up to peruse the city unfolding around us and then back to the map. "I can set it into motion. I'd have more pull if this was our dimension, but..." He looked around again and then focused on what looked like a foot bridge hanging high above the streets. From the ribbon of glistening blue snaking along below it, I presumed the walkway stretched over a river. "...I'll talk to Madeline. I don't care if this is the demonic plane, an agent of the government should never be allowed to mistreat a helpless creature like that."

I turned to find the little green furball kissing Hobs's nose and grinned before I could stop myself. The creature's scruffy tail was wagging so hard I could hear it smacking against Hobs's white tunic. "It sure is cute."

Bandy Joe slid a suspicious gaze over the creature. "Yes. It doesn't seem to belong in this wretched place."

He wasn't wrong.

"Come on," Grym said, wrapping his hand around my arm in a gentle grip. "We need to go this way."

"How do you know?" I asked.

He held the map up and showed me a cluster of the unfamiliar symbols that resembled a spider. As I watched, the spider moved, heading across the hanging walkway. "Is that the piper?"

"Yep," Grym said.

I grinned. "We got him!"

14

YOUR HEAD NO LONGER HAS A HOLE IN IT. YOU'RE GOOD

Of course, it wasn't going to be as easy as chasing a small moving clump of demonic symbols that I assumed spelled "piper" across a map. While we pursued the slowly-moving script, we also had to navigate through New Baal.

No easy task, that.

"We should have worn disguises," I mumbled to Grym as a crowd of truly horrifying creatures moved in on us, their gazes a mix of aggression, rage, and intrusive curiosity.

I don't know what I'd been expecting, probably something along the lines of the no-name snake-tailed guy we'd left behind in the Keeper's office. But the reality was just so much more colorful than I could have imagined.

Apparently, demons came in all types, shapes, and sizes. Not all had horns or tails. Many didn't even have claws. A few had humanoid forms but most didn't. Whatever shape they took, they all had one thing in common.

None of them could be mistaken for human.

But we could. And, unluckily for us, they seemed fascinated to see us there.

Apparently they didn't get a lot of human tourists in New Baal.

Grym kept us moving through the non-descript, unimaginative streets despite the furor we created wherever we went.

Hurrying down one street, we were cut off by something that looked like a spider through the body but walked upright on two of its eight legs. Its face had pincers for a mouth and three sets of glossy black eyes. As we tried to move around the creature, it advanced on Hobs and reached for him. The little green creature in his arms growled, showing a lot of teeth when it opened its tiny mouth.

The spider demon jerked its leg away and reared back.

Watch out! Slimy yelled in my head. *It's doing something.*

I grabbed for Hobs, intending to yank him behind me. I needn't have bothered. The hobgoblin moved away so quickly the nasty, goo-coated web the thing shot at him hung in the air with nowhere to go for a beat before sagging toward the ground.

After that, we walked more quickly, Grym

constantly reminding us not to run. "A lot of these things love to chase, and they aren't gentle when they catch," he warned.

"You sound like you speak from experience," I said.

He sighed. "Unfortunately, I do. Years ago, before you came to Croakies, we had a demon problem in Enchanted. I was a brand new cop back then, so I was considered too green to deal with them. But I watched some really good cops go down under these things. It stuck with me."

I frowned. "But the Enchanted police force is mostly human, right?"

He nodded. "When I joined, there were a lot more supernormal people on the force. A lot of them ended up moving to larger cities, where the supernormal forces were larger and they had better funding." He grinned down at me. "They thought Enchanted was too boring."

I barked out a laugh.

"*My* Enchanted is all supernormals," Bandy Joe said. "It makes life much simpler."

I thought of some of my favorite non-magic customers at the book store and realized I'd miss them. "I don't know. Humans give us a different perspective. I think it's important to have a mix." Not to mention, I'd thought I was a non-magic human for the first eighteen years of my life. I knew first-hand what it felt like to not have magic. Since experiencing the supernormal world, I'd discovered that life was more interesting with magic. But that didn't make non-magic life less precious.

Incoming! Slimy yelled.

We all ducked as something whipped by just above our heads. The monstrous bird zeroed in on me, its claws scraping across my arms and hands.

Grym reached up and punched the thing as it tried to snatch the fat squish from my hands.

Ah! No! Eeeeeep! Slimy screamed in a loop that ratcheted higher with every swipe of the deadly claws.

Grym punched the flying creature two more times and it finally lifted away, screaming its rage before flapping ragged black wings and flying toward the distant skyline.

"Ouch!" I said, examining the long, bloody scratches on my arms. "You okay, Mr. Slimy?"

I'm minus a little pee, but otherwise alright.

I grimaced at the puddle on my palm. *Yeah. I'm aware.*

Hey, pee happens.

Around you, it seems to happen a lot.

"Did you see the beak on that thing?" Bandy Joe asked. He reached into his pocket and pulled out a small metal box I hadn't known he'd grabbed from the artifact library.

"You brought Florence Nightingale's med kit." I handed Slimy to Grym.

"I hope you don't mind. It seemed like a good idea."

As Joe tended my arms for me, I asked Grym if we'd lost the piper.

"He stopped moving after he crossed the bridge. But, we need to find a way to travel faster if we hope to catch him." Grym glanced around, staring at a shop window up the street from where we stood. The front was all glass and inside the windows was an assortment of strange-looking clothes. He pointed to a bench against a nearby building. A couple of strange-looking trees hung over the bench, the shade and trees creating a little haven where we could stay out of sight. "Sit down over there for a few minutes. Try to be inconspicuous." He grinned. "I'll be right back."

"You need backup," I insisted.

He shook his head. "I'll be fine. Sit. Stay."

"Woof!" I called after him, earning a smile from my cop.

Bandy Joe and I sat down on the bench. Hobs and the furry creature went behind the bench and played a game of picking up the strange-looking flowers decorating the dark gray concrete beneath us.

I sat and stared out at the city, a sense of excitement building as I really saw it for the first time. A sense of awe temporarily eclipsed the dangerous quality of the experience. New Baal was huge, the chaotic lines of its architecture painting the sky as far as the eye could see.

Residents moved and shopped and visited along its maze of streets, infusing the cityscape with a pleasant sense of movement and productivity that was about as far away from what I'd anticipated as it could be.

The streets we'd crossed had been lined on both sides in short, blocky buildings with narrow alleys between them. All of the taller buildings, the ones with the aggressive architecture Grym had noted, were clustered at the very center of the city. I guessed that was probably where the financial and government districts were located. The seat of all the power.

Where we were, the residents were dressed plainly in rough-looking robes and loose trousers. The women wore scarves that hung over their faces like a bill on a baseball cap. Many of the men wore a type of hat I'd never seen before. It was wide-brimmed and sat low on their heads, fitting their skulls closely, but the brim was split so that it resembled a flower, its petals stretching up to eight inches away from the main part of the hat. Between the petals was a gauzy material that I assumed was there for ventilation. It was certainly hot in New Baal.

Deadly hot.

I was glad for the shaded bench and the chance to rest and cool off. It was really pleasant too. For about five minutes. Then something small, furry, and black launched itself from the tree and smacked into me, claws and teeth slashing even as it landed on my head.

I screeched as the thing ripped at my hair, chittering as it pulled out strand after strand. Bandy Joe screamed too, his bulky body writhing and jerking on the bench as he tried to punch a second squirrel-like creature away from his head and face.

A gust of Hobs-scented air whipped over me, and the demonic squirrel that had been on my head was suddenly gone.

The small green demon-dog leaped into the air, its jaws clamping over the manic squirrel attacking Joe and flinging it away. Hobs returned a beat later, his passage toward us visible only as a blur of white on the air.

"Are you okay, Miss?"

I gingerly felt along my scalp where the creature had ripped out my hair. "I don't think my hair's okay. But I guess I am." I looked at Joe. He had a bloody gash on the top of his head. It glistened through his shorter hair, more visible than my own wounds. "You alright?"

He was already pulling out the medkit. "I'm fine. I'd heard about squirrel demons. But everything I've heard says they're harmless. Much like the squirrels in our dimensions."

Hobs patted my arm soothingly. "They didn't

mean any harm, Miss. Vel says they're just feathering their nests."

I stared at him, confused. "Vel?"

Hobs's face split in a wide smile. "My friend." He pointed to the green, doglike creature sitting on the concrete in front of us, tail wagging. There was a pile of the flowers they'd been gathering in front of her. She barked, the sound a little gravelly on the edges but otherwise like a regular dog's bark.

"I've seen these flowers before, Miss. They have healing magic."

My eyes went wide. I stared down at the tiny blossoms with their waxy white petals and velvety purple centers with yellow stamen. Vel barked again and shoved the pile of flowers with her wet, brown nose.

Reaching for the blooms, I held them in my palm and looked a question at Bandy Joe.

He shrugged. "I'll go first."

I watched as he took half the blossoms and popped them into his mouth. His bulgy black eyes went wide and his throat worked over the blooms, making him look even more like his favorite reptiles than usual.

His round face twitched. A beat later, one of his cheeks bulged outward. Bandy Joe made a strangled kind of noise, and I jumped to my feet. I reached for the medkit, not sure what I was going to do with it, but sensing that something was about to go terribly wrong. Silvery magic oozed from my palms, swirling lazily around us as it searched for a purpose.

I yelped as the other side of Bandy Joe's face bulged outward, his head swelled, turning conical, and his jaw got sucked into his face.

His features writhed and rolled for a long moment, and his thick body twitched with alarm at every change, his eyes impossibly wide. By the time everything settled back into place, I was a nervous wreck, my heart pounding against my ribs.

I couldn't imagine how he felt.

The good news was that the wound on his head was gone.

Horrified silence hung between us for a beat, and then I looked at my bleeding arms and said, "I'm good. These scratches are fine. It's all good."

Joe narrowed his gaze on me. "Seriously? I went through all that for nothing?"

"Not nothing. Your head no longer has a hole in it. You're good. I'm good. It's all good." I knew I sounded kind of manic, but there was no way I was eating those flowers. I was going to have nightmares for years over the sight of his fluctuating face.

Joe grabbed the flowers from my palm and slid them into his pocket. When I gave him a horrified look, he shrugged. "For experimental purposes only."

I shook my head.

"Okay," Grym said from directly behind me.

"Ah!" I whipped around, slashing ineffectually with my hands, and received a quizzical arch of one brow from the gargoyle.

"Did something happen while I was gone?" he asked in a sardonic tone.

I patted my squirrel-scrambled hair and shook my head. "Nope. It's all good."

Hobs opened his mouth, but I glared at him. He snapped it shut.

Joe's mouth opened and a thunderous belch emerged, leaving behind an atrocious sulfuric stench.

"Ah!" I exclaimed, covering my nose and moving away from him.

"Sorry," Joe said, glaring at me. "Something I ate must have disagreed with me."

I warned him to silence with a wide-eyed gaze.

"Woof!" Vel bounced happily around Grym's feet, tail wagging.

Grym smiled down at the cute little creature.

"What's that?" Bandy Joe asked, clearly trying to change the subject. He pointed toward the oversized bag in Grym's hand.

Grym dug his hand into the bag, pulling out a pile of rough cloth and handing it to me. "These are robes like everyone is wearing. I thought we could make better time if we didn't stick out so much."

I smiled at the oversized hood on the robe he'd given me. It would keep me safe from jumbo-sized demon birds *and* nasty squirrel demons. I threw the robe over my head, happy to see that its long sleeves hid the fading scratch marks on my arms. Joe and Grym did the same. Their robes were a dark brown, nearly black, and mine was a dirty tan color.

"We'll want to move fast," Grym said. "I didn't get the loose trousers, so they might notice our jeans."

We nodded in agreement, and Grym pulled out the map. He eyed the flashing spider that was the Pied Piper, frowning.

"What's wrong?" I asked.

"He's moved again. I can't make out what this place is. There's a dome of some kind."

Hobs moved closer and peered down at the map. He pointed a finger at the spidery image. "That's the music center. They have music and stuff outside. I saw Snow White and the Seven Demons there once. It was fun."

I felt my eyes widen. "Music Center?" Grym and Joe looked every bit as worried as I did.

"We need to go!" I said, taking off running toward the bridge. Hobs shot past us before we'd gone a block, a white blur with a green center. "Vel and I will scope it out, Miss," he called back to me as he shot past.

"No, Hobs!" As usual, he ignored me. But my call had drawn the gazes of several demons. Interest flared in their scary eyes. I clamped my lips shut and ran faster. Prey drive or not. We couldn't dally any longer.

The worst possible thing that could happen while we were in New Baal would be for the creature we were tracking to create a local incident by luring a bunch of New Baaleans to their deaths.

15

CAN YOU READ THESE ETCHINGS?

Hobs was nowhere to be found by the time we hit the hanging walkway. Our intention to hurry was brutally severed the moment we realized the bridge didn't respond well to speed. It lurched into a hammock-like swing beneath our feet, nearly flinging us and about a dozen other walkers to the roiling waters below.

A chorus of husky shouts met our antics, and we were forced to slow, murmuring apologies. Clinging to the main cable for extra support, we walked as quickly as we could. By the time we stepped off the end of the bridge onto solid ground, I could hear the sounds of tuning instruments in the distance. We took off running again, heading for the clamshell-shaped structure ahead. We jolted to a halt at the edge of the gathered crowd, and Grym perused the magical map.

I looked over his shoulder as Bandy Joe huffed like a buffalo behind us. The spidery cluster of symbols that was the piper had gone still, immersed within the massive crowd of demons standing, sitting, and milling about on the grounds of the musical amphitheater. "Where is he?" I asked Grym.

He frowned over the map, tension evident in his big frame despite the obscuring fabric of the robe. "I don't know." He lifted his head. "We'll need to split up and move through the throng."

I stared at the massive crowd and felt my mouth go dry. It would be a huge undertaking. But beyond that, the thought of being in the middle of hundreds of demons with no real way to defend myself if it went pear-shaped was intimidating.

"I'll take the middle," Grym was saying.

Bandy Joe nodded toward the far side. "I'll walk along the tree line there."

I started toward the remaining side, taking care to keep the hood low over my face and to stay as far away from every creature in my path as possible. I searched for the piper and Hobs at the same time. The little hobgoblin would make my search easier.

I was nearly to the stage when I felt a little tickle in my magical core. I'd felt that tickle before, when I'd gotten close to a rogue magical artifact.

Releasing a tentative stream of Keeper magic, I waited, searching for movement in the crowd. I felt someone watching me and tried to huddle deeper into my robe. The soft whoosh of sound was all the warning I got. I stuck my hand into the air, and a knife with a curved blade slapped into my palm. I sucked air as the double-edged athame sliced into my fingers.

There was a gasp as the woman next to me spotted the artifact. "She has a knife!" the demon screamed.

The group around me became agitated, jostling each other in an attempt to shift away.

I shook my head, making the knife disappear beneath my robe, and tried to slip through the crowd.

I wasn't fast enough.

"Stop, thief!" yelled someone from the midst of the gathering. "She stole my ceremonial blade."

Several large forms turned in my direction. Several pairs of multi-hued eyes fixed on me. Fangs emerged from between downturned lips and tense jaws. Fists clenched.

I swallowed hard, backing slowly away. "I...um..."

The huge demons stalked after me.

Buzzard butts!

I turned and took off running, knowing there was no way I'd be able to talk my way out of the current kerfuffle.

A familiar hand grabbed me, long fingers curling tightly around mine. "This way, Miss."

Hobs put on the speed, and the world became a

blur. When we finally stopped, I rocked in place, my eyes crossed, and my vision skewed. "I'll never get used to that," I told the little hobgoblin.

He grinned up at me.

"Woof!"

I crouched down to give Vel a scratch under her chin. "I've been looking for you guys," I said in a baby voice to Vel. "Yes, I have."

"Woof!" she said again, dancing from paw to paw with obvious excitement.

I straightened. "Did you find the piper?" I asked Hobs.

"No, Miss. We lost him in the crowd."

I eyed the little demon dog. "Do you suppose Vel could sniff him out?"

Hobs shrugged. "If we had something of his we could use to set her on his trail."

I deflated. He was right. I couldn't ask the little dog to sniff out something we couldn't identify. Sighing, I extracted the blade from the folds of my robe so I could look at it. The black handle had carvings along its length, which continued onto the ten-inch blade. I showed it to Hobs. "Can you read these etchings?"

Hobs stared at it for a long moment and then shook his head. "No, Miss. It looks like an ancient form of demonish." He scrunched up his pert nose, pointing to a symbol that was repeated several times along its length. The character looked like an elongated S, severed in the center by a hatchet with a curved blade. Each end of the S was a serpent's head, their forked tongues tasting the air and the slanted eyes pinched closed as if from pain.

Hobs pointed to the figure. "This is similar to a modern symbol that means to cut," he said.

That was hardly a life-changing observation, given that it was a knife and knives were predominantly known for cutting.

I hid it back in my robe as the crowd around us started to grow agitated again. There was a loud popping noise. My gaze shot toward the sound, and I saw a small man standing on the stage, bending over the microphone. "Hello! Welcome."

The crowd cheered.

I slid my gaze over the gathering, wondering where Grym and Joe had ended up. Hopefully, they'd had better luck finding the piper.

"Thanks for coming to *The Magic of Music* tonight. You're in for a real treat!" said the man on the stage. He skimmed a sharp cobalt gaze over the crowd and settled it on the spot where we stood.

My pulse spiked as he looked directly into my eyes and...winked.

"Hobs...?"

The hobgoblin grabbed my wrist, and I tensed for the quick jolt of his magic dragging me away. But it never came. Several things happened at once.

First, the man on the stage pulled a long, wooden

object with holes along its length from his pocket. Second, magic swirled from the pipe and spun on the air, a tiny whirlwind of silver and purple motes that spread quickly through the crowd. I watched in horror as the Pied Piper's deadly magic sifted into the assembled demons' nostrils and open mouths as they gave a preemptory cheer in anticipation of the music to come. Third, the piper lifted the instrument to his lips and began to play.

"No!" I took off running for the stage, screaming Grym's name as I ran. The crowd split around me at first, flinging angry glances my way and even, in a few cases, making an angry grab for me. I ducked and wove and held an unwavering path toward the pale-haired man with the overlarge teeth. I watched in horror as his delicate fingers danced over the magical instrument with practiced ease.

Music as fine and gentle as an angelic chorus danced on the air around us, each note an intoxicating enticement, impossible to ignore. It pulled at me, a gentle temptation that fogged my mind and stripped me of the reason for my previous rush.

I jolted to a stop, the graceful notes an enchanting buffet of musical delicacies. I pulled air into my lungs and savored its taste, feeling my body swell and my mind soften under the melody's deft touch. Without realizing it, I began to sway along with the entranced crowd.

In the distance, someone called my name.

No. Not my name, a familiar address. *Miss! Miss! Miss!*

Hobs. Yes, it was Hobs. Why was he bothering me? I shook my head as if trying to shake off a persistent fly buzzing around my ears.

Pebbles skittered away from my feet. Grass crushed beneath my shoes, sending up a sweet scent that melded into the golden notes on the air to create my perfect moment. Someone jostled me from behind, their shoving hand impatient and filled with an urgency I couldn't fathom.

The toe of my sneaker struck a rock and I stumbled slightly, the press of those behind me sending me off the path. My head connected with a tree and pain yanked me from the music's grip. I staggered, blinked, and shook my head as confusion turned my thoughts to slush. My knees buckled and I went down. When my mind finally cleared, I saw that I was lying mere inches from the brink. Far below, the water crashed and spun and sent mist into the air, its mood as chaotic as my thoughts.

I slid my gaze along the walkway, seeing the press of bodies on the weaving planks. The demons were packed shoulder to shoulder and moving slowly. Already, the structure was groaning loudly, its main cable straining to hold what had to be hundreds of demons at one time.

At that moment, I realized all those people were

about to die. The suspended walkway was going to give out at any minute.

My horrified gaze found a large, dark-haired man in the very center of the bridge, and my stomach twisted in alarm.

Grym!

I shot to my feet, scanning the distance for the source of the compelling music.

The piper stood on a bench on the opposite side of the walkway, sending his lethal music into the air. He was perfectly safe from the destruction he was about to cause.

I opened my mouth and started to scream, praying it would be enough to jolt the masses out of their compelled state.

A blur of white and green flashed past, leaving behind a disembodied apology I recognized all too well. "Hobs, no!"

But he ignored me. As the cable on the suspended walkway gave a terrifying twang, unable to sustain the type of weight the piper had lured onto its planks, I panicked. My mind raced, fear making it hard to think. Running out onto the bridge would only add to the weight problem. But I couldn't just watch it happen, either. So I gritted my teeth and stepped onto the walkway behind the last row of coerced music lovers.

The walkway gave a violent lurch as one of the cables splintered. I sucked air and grabbed the handrails in a white-knuckled grip. In desperation mode, I smacked the nearest demon on the back with my open palm.

To my relief, the man jerked to a stop, shook his head, and whipped around to glare at me, baring his fangs and growling.

I held up my hands, calling as much Keeper magic as I could rip from my core. "You're all being compelled. The walkway is going to break. Everyone will be killed."

The rage slowly bled from his black eyes.

"We need to get these people off the bridge."

His toothy mouth snapped shut, and he gave me a quick nod. He turned and grabbed a woman holding a baby, pushing her at me, and then dove forward, slapping each demon he encountered in the head none too gently.

I pulled the woman off the bridge and gave her a little shove toward the amphitheater. "Sit in the grass and stay," I barked at her, having no idea if my instruction would even sink in.

As I turned, three more demons stumbled off the bridge and collapsed into the grass.

The demon I'd recruited to help had gotten several others to help, and they were turning people back at a steady if too-slow rate.

Another wrench of the walkway threw people toward the handrails. Screaming ensued, and the demons who'd been woken started to run as panic set in.

I continued to move farther onto the walkway, one eye on the raging water and jagged rocks below. I guided people off the foot bridge, running to help a child and an older woman when they were pushed to the ground in the headlong rush, nearly getting trampled.

As I delivered the child to a hysterical woman on shore, I heard Grym screaming my name and realized he thought I was on the walkway. I screamed back, waving my arms until he spotted me. "Get people off that thing!" I yelled.

He nodded. Picking two small kids up under one arm and grabbing their mother around the waist, he started to run toward the grass.

Another cable twanged and then broke, the walkway tilting dangerously. A man fell over the handrail, a husky scream vibrating on his lips. Bandy Joe threw himself at the rail and grabbed the man's arm. The demon thrashed and fought, fear getting the best of him. Joe was nearly pulled over by the demon, who was fighting to gain a foothold on a limp cable near his feet. Rather than hold his weight, the cable fell away from him and dangled toward the frothy water below.

Finally, two demons, both much larger than Joe, stepped up on either side of him to help. Between them, they managed to pull the man back onto the walkway.

Another cable gave. Screams sliced the dusky light and the demons' panic increased. The screams of terror were mixed with shrieks of pain as people were trampled in the melee. I stood on a flat-topped rock near the walkway, trying to see if the piper was still there. It was getting hard to hear the music beneath the screams and the pounding of feet on the planks.

He still stood on the bench, the magical pipe between his lips and a mad gleam in his eyes.

The crowd on the grass had grown considerably. But as I looked out over the bodies left on the suspension bridge, I knew too many would die.

A familiar blur swept past the piper, and the villain's hands were suddenly empty. He looked around, blinking in confusion as the blur shot along the handrails in my direction.

Hobs!

The main cable groaned and started to fray in a succession of nerve-scraping twangs. The walkway dropped in a quick series of violent jerks, and the chaos on its planks rose to a fever pitch.

Hobs skidded to a stop next to me, handing me the pipe.

I grabbed him into a hug. "You could have been killed."

"No, Miss, I was safe."

I hugged him again.

"Naida!" My gaze snapped up and I waved the pipe at Grym. "Just get them all off."

He turned to say something to Joe and several other demons who'd been helping to rouse people from their stupors.

A moment later, they started to drive the remaining people toward the closest end. With the piper out of commission, they had a much better chance of surviving the quickly unraveling bridge going that way.

But people were panicked, and they ran Grym and the others right over in an attempt to get back to the amphitheater.

The cable groaned long and loud, and the section of walkway nearest me plunged downward, jerking to a stop only when the cable snapped up and got caught on a thick branch of an overhanging tree.

I turned to the demons behind me. "I need as many of you as are able to come help me hold this cable."

I expected argument or reluctance, but a dozen big guys ran over and nudged me out of the way, quickly anchoring the cable around the thick trunk of the tree and then lining up to hold onto it.

I ran toward the walkway and forced myself to step down onto it. No longer anchored, it swung in a way that made my stomach flip and twist. Taking a deep breath, I threw up my hands and screamed for the people to go the other way.

They kept coming, practically assuring their own deaths.

Suddenly a small, green creature shot out from between their legs and ran to a spot several yards ahead of the fleeing demons. I watched in horror as Vel's tail whipped twice and tears filled my eyes. She'd either be trampled or killed when the cables finally gave out. "Vel, come!"

She wagged her tail but otherwise ignored me.

The demon dog opened her mouth. And opened it. And opened it.

I gasped as her jaws seemed to unhinge and spread until her mouth was as big as she was. In front of her, footsteps slowed and faltered at the sight.

"Go back!" I screamed. "Hurry." But they didn't move. Their gazes were locked on Vel.

Banshee bellows and bat boogers! I swore.

A deep, primal roar, not unlike what we'd experienced too many times when we'd visited the Jurassic period and gotten temporarily stuck there, filled the air. Along with Vel's impossible roar, a gush of visible wind rushed out of her supersized mouth, literally blowing people back and away.

That finally got through to them. The remaining mass of demons on the walkway turned on their heels and started to run, too terrified even to scream.

They didn't get far. The cable finally gave way on the far end, forcing Grym and Joe and the other men back toward my end of the bridge. With a final screech of tearing metal and shattering wood, the final third of the walkway began to plunge toward the rocks far below. The center sagged downward but held, and people swung around, fleeing back toward me with faces that were pale as paper and filled with terror.

I turned to the guys holding the cable in place. "We need more people here!" I screamed and ran to grab the cable as more demons surrounded me and found spots to grab.

The center dropped several inches. People screamed as the back half of the crowd fell to their knees or clutched at the cable as they were pressed backward by the hysterical crowd. Grym and some of the other men grabbed those who were in danger of falling, yanking them back and pushing them forward just as the last cable in the center broke. The segment plunged downward, metal squealing and wood splintering as it plummeted toward the river.

But not all of the section made it to the water.

My end of the walkway was wrenched as something in the middle section got caught on it, yanking it violently from side to side as it swung mostly free.

We were jerked forward and then thrown back

under the strain. I fell to my knees, joined by many others who weren't heavy enough to fight the pull.

Vel ran from the walkway and joined me, whining pitifully down by my feet. "Good girl," I told the little demon, earning a quick whip of her tail.

All that was left was the section we were holding up with our bare hands. The line of support grew silent as we all grasped what was coming our way.

I looked down the line at the tense expressions and felt a swell of pride to be part of it. I'd never think badly of the demonic realm again.

The cable holding the back of our section screeched, the metal twisting slowly under all the weight.

"Run!" Grym screamed, spurring the crowd to pick up the pace. But it was nearly impossible to run with the walkway blowing back and forth under the effects of the unmoored section waving on the wind.

As the crowd started to hit solid ground, I gave myself a moment of hope that they'd all make it. Given that Grym would be one of the last ones off, I needed to believe that more than anything.

Our line was jerked hard. We all stumbled forward as the anchor started to give out, and the cable sliced through the thick branch as it slowly unwound.

"Hold!" someone screamed.

Grunts and growls filled the air as the men dug in. But their feet skidded along the grass, digging tracks in the soil as they were yanked toward the edge.

"We need to lose the center section," one of them screamed.

He was right. We could probably hold against the weight of the people, but that loose section was wrenching everything and making it impossible to hold on.

My mind swam, trying to come up with a solution. Something niggled my brain. Something that had happened within the last few minutes. Something that might help...

It clicked. I plunged a hand into the pocket I'd found in a fold of my robe and stepped away from the cable line, getting into an open space.

"Miss?"

I glanced at Hobs. "Stay clear."

"The knife, Miss!"

I didn't comment. He'd come to the same conclusion I had. I simply nodded, braced myself on the edge of the ridge, and said a quick prayer that we'd all survive.

Then I lifted my hands in the air, clutching the knife, and filled my mind with what I needed. I had no idea if that was the right thing to do, but I was an artifact keeper, and the knife was an artifact. Technically, it should be under my control.

So I'd control it.

I sent as much keeper energy into the knife as I

could, focusing on sending the magic from the artifact rather than calling it.

Then I looked toward the spot I was trying to affect and flung out the hand with the knife.

"Sever!" I yelled, not knowing if it even needed to be vocalized. My gut churning with fear that I'd sever the wrong thing, I watched the magic surge out of the blade and shoot toward the spot where the fallen section swung wildly through the air. The magic sliced through the hanging section like a hot knife through butter and, with a final screech of wood against metal, it plummeted downward toward the angry river.

The section of walkway crashed into the river, a wall of water exploding into the air as the debris sank out of view.

The following silence seemed almost violent after the upheaval of the previous moments. Everyone seemed a bit shell-shocked.

Then, the crowd appeared to realize it wasn't over yet, and the rest of the demons on the walkway started running again. I sagged with relief as the last of them limped, pale-faced and panting, off the still-swinging planks.

Out of nowhere came a melodic whistle that somehow rose above the noise of hundreds of people talking excitedly and crying. The infectious sound danced across the gaping ravine toward me.

My head shot up, and I found myself staring at

the pale, slender man across the abyss. He gave me a smile and a salute, one hand snapping up and closing into a fist above his head. Then he disappeared into thin air.

The piper was gone.

16

9-1-1! 9-1-1!

It was a defeated ragtag group who stepped back onto the concrete floor at Croakies. Except, of course, for the hobgoblin and his new bestie, Vel. They were thrilled just to be alive.

I watched them take off across the artifact library and opened my mouth to warn Hobs to keep the demon dog away from the artifacts, then closed it as they disappeared around the end of the shelves.

I was too tired for that battle.

"Meow!" Wicked trotted out of the shadows and rammed into my legs, purring and scolding me at the same time.

"Hey, buddy," I said, scooping him up. "I missed you too."

"We should get the pipe into the toxic magic vault," Grym reminded me. "We can talk about how to find the piper again over dinner."

I perked up a bit. "Dinner?"

He grinned. "My treat. It's meatloaf night at the diner down the street."

My stomach rumbled, and my mouth started to water at the same time. "Sounds good."

Bandy Joe headed toward the book store with zoom sitting on his head and Slimy carefully cradled in his big hands. "I'll get these little beasties settled and fed."

"Thanks, Joe," I said, reaching into the pocket inside my robe.

My hand hit rough cloth and nothing else. Panic flared. I must have made a sound because Grym moved closer. "What's wrong?"

I yanked the robe off and turned it inside out, squeezing the fabric on both sides just in case I'd put the pipe into the wrong pocket.

"Naida, what's wrong?"

Tears of frustration burned my eyes. Panic made my heart pound.

Grym touched my arm, "Naida?"

I looked up, my face wet with tears. "It's gone. The pipe's gone."

He was silent as I continued to slap helplessly at the robe. Finally, I dropped it and rubbed my hands over my face. "I lost it. I can't believe I lost it."

I sank to the floor in total despair. We'd blown through two days of the three King Rhorr had given us. We had less than twenty-four hours to find the pipe and get the piper. Less than one day.

I buried my face in my hands. I'd failed.

Grym dropped down onto the floor, his warmth wrapping around me. He pulled me against his chest. "Do you think it fell out of your pocket? I can go back and see if I can find it."

Even the thought of going back to New Baal made my bones melt with weariness. "It could have fallen out anywhere." We'd walked a long way after losing the piper to reach a second walkway over the river and get back to where we'd lost him. We'd had a vague hope of Vel sniffing him out, but the little dog had tracked him to a wall and lost his scent. We had to have covered miles of the city in our search.

Then a memory surfaced that made me go very still.

The melodic whistle that impossibly could be heard above the noise of hundreds of people, its infectious sound dancing across the gaping ravine toward me.

Magic.

The pale, slender man across the abyss who gave me a smile and a salute then reached up and snagged something from the air above his head before disappearing into thin air.

My hopes sank. "I know where it is."

Grym released me so he could look into my face. "Where?"

Expelling a burst of frustrated air, I shook my head. "The Piper has it. He magicked it away from me just before he disappeared." I sagged downward. "We've lost them both."

I was too stressed out to go to dinner. Grym insisted I needed to eat something, so he left with the promise to bring dinner back. I barely heard him leave. I was seated at Shakespeare's desk, searching out books that could help me find the Piper before he hurt anyone else.

I wondered what Sebille was doing. And Rustin. Hopefully, whatever they were up to, they were having better success than I was.

I forced my mind away from other things, needing to focus on the direct problem.

I had to find the piper even more than the pipe, which was just a hunk of varnished wood with holes in it. Without the piper, the pipe was at least temporarily neutered.

I needed to get it back and lock it up. But my deal with King Rhorr and the safety of the people of Enchanted depended on getting the piper.

That was what I'd focus on.

Having made the decision, I felt better. "Desk, I need everything you have on tracking magic. Particularly tracking magic that will cross dimensions."

The leather blotter under my hands was carved to look like a book cover, with the Shakespeare family crest on the spine. At my request, it warmed under my fingers, and the leather rolled beneath my palms. A moment later, a small, canvas-bound book popped into existence above the desk. I pulled it from the air and started reading as the desk continued to search.

I was deep into the third resource book when the bell over the front door in the bookstore jangled. I frowned, knowing the store was closed and the door had been locked.

It had to be Sebille, returning from her secret adventure. I kept reading, knowing that she'd find me if she wanted to.

A few moments later, I heard movement in from the store. Cocking one ear toward the door handle, I waited for her to come through.

Something thudded to the ground from that direction. My gaze shot to the door. Another loud thud had me jumping to my feet.

911! 911! screamed the frog inside my head.

What's wrong? I asked him.

Bring the sword! he responded unhelpfully.

I threw out my Keeper magic, and there was a clatter high above my head. Hearing the soft swish of something flying through the air, I lifted my hand just as a heavy sword found my palm.

The hilt of Blackbeard's sword warmed and

shifted, molding to fit my grip even as the weight of the large weapon adjusted itself so I could wield it easily.

Wings flapped clumsily above me, and a long green feather drifted lazily to the ground, its edges frayed and the color dull with age. "Bwawk!!" the parrot squawked. "Beware the bleepin' villain. Run the blackguard through."

Sewer Beak, or SB for short, had ridden Blackbeard's shoulder for long enough to permanently color his language. The problem was bad enough that he was no longer fit for polite company. Alice, the previous Keeper of the Artifacts at Croakies, had him bespelled to bleep his more colorful language. But the spirit of the words still managed to shine through within the context of his speech.

"That's the idea," I told him, giving the blade a few warmup swings. The arc of my swing barely missed the clumsily flapping parrot's wings, causing him to rise into the air with another outraged squawk. "Bleep, bleep, and bleepity bleep! Take care ye bilge rat. Ye'll give me a rullock on me dungbie!" I knew enough of pirate speak to know he'd just called me an idiot and accused me of trying to cut a notch in his backside. I did a mental shrug. A notch or two in the foul-mouthed bird might not be a bad idea. It might take some of the starch out of his undead attitude.

I started toward the dividing door, pirate energy

making my steps as light as if I were traversing a ship's deck on a rolling sea.

I threw open the door and stepped into the store, my sword held at the ready. The entrance would have been more intimidating if it weren't for the out-of-control ball of squawks and feathers that tumbled through after me.

A soft chuckle brought my head up. My intruder stood in front of the picture window overlooking the street in front of Croakies. At his feet were several large volumes, clearly thrown to the floor in an attempt to catch my attention.

I glared at the slight man, who looked to be several inches shorter than my five feet nine inches, with narrow hips and shoulders. In the illumination filtering through the window from the streetlight beyond the glass, I could see he had light brown hair that was carelessly tousled on his small head. I couldn't tell the color of his almost-too-large eyes in the low light, but I was pretty sure they were cobalt blue. He stood straight, appearing relaxed, and held a pipe in one small hand. "Naida keeper. Such a pleasure to finally meet you."

The sword's energy thrummed along my fingers and arms, anxious to slice and dice. It was hard to think past that desire, and I fought the urge to clear my mind by shaking my head. I glanced quickly toward Slimy's aquarium, finding him and Zoom blinking at me, unharmed.

What do you see? I asked the frog.

He's holding a lot of magic right now. It's pulsing around him like a shield.

The piper cocked his head, his gaze sliding to the aquarium and a small smile forming on his lips. "Fascinating. Do they both speak to you?"

I forced myself not to glance at the frogs. "I don't know what you're talking about."

The piper laughed. "I'm sure you do not."

"What do you want?" I asked the evil little man. "Why are you here?"

"I should think that would be obvious. I've returned for the 1,000 guilders you owe me."

That caught me off guard. I thought back over what Endeara had told me about dimensional crimping. Was the piper really confused about who I was and which city he was tormenting? It didn't seem possible. "This isn't Hamelin, I told him. And I'm not the mayor who cheated you. I understand why you'd be unhappy about that, but none of the people you've hurt had anything to do with it."

"Neither did the children of Hamelin, yet they suffered for it just the same."

Gooseflesh slid along my arms. I thought about Endeara's vision of the piper leading Enchanted's children away, and the small hairs on the back of my neck stood at attention. The unprepossessing figure in front of me was pure evil. A magical sociopath who'd stop at nothing to get what he wanted. "Why now?" I asked. "That was hundreds of years ago."

He squinted at me as if I were deranged. "Was it? It is here and now in my mind. As near as this morning and as close as those delightful reptiles. The dimension isn't the only thing that folds, dear Keeper. Time is as malleable as space. Do not ever forget that."

I gave up trying to understand what brought him to our doorstep at that moment. Ultimately, it didn't really matter. He was standing in front of me, and he'd given me a path out of the current mess. "I'll need a few hours to get the money together."

"One thousand guilders," he said sharply, as if suspecting me of pulling a fast one.

"One thousand guilders," I repeated. "I am not the Mayor of Hamelin. I won't cheat you."

"Ah," he said, a tight smile on his golden face. "That rascal promised me the same. But I'll take you at your word. Only if you bring him to me with the coins."

"Huh? Bring who?"

"Do not play me for a fool!" he shouted, all semblance of sanity cast aside. "The white-haired beast whose people I compelled. He thought I could not see his true form beneath the monstrous disguise. I'd know my nemesis anywhere. Bring that one to me in chains along with the coin, and I will return those who you love."

I blinked in surprise. "Wait? Those who I love? What are you talking about?"

His response was to put the pipe between his lips and start to play.

Naida! Slimy screamed in my head.

Ribbit! Zoom belched, his orange eyes bulging with fear.

The two frogs rose from the aquarium and floated to the piper, who stood in front of the open front door.

The dividing door behind me was flung open too, crashing back against the wall. Hobs and Baca walked out, their eyes glazed and their movements wooden.

Inside my head, I screamed. But my body wouldn't move.

Beyond the glass, I watched as Lea shambled down the sidewalk, zombified by the piper's music. Queen Sindra and a long line of her fae fell into line behind Lea. Rustin and Sadie came out of the building across the street and fell into line with the others.

Carrying several large paper bags, Grym and Bandy Joe fell into step behind the fae, having apparently just arrived with dinner. The piper's music was a series of broken notes and squeals in my ears. It didn't draw me as it had before. Instead, it locked my feet into place, incapacitating my limbs so I could only watch in terror as Fenwald, Mr.

Wicked, and Hex, his sister from next door, joined the line.

The piper hadn't lied. He'd taken everyone I loved.

I might end up being the only one left to stop him.

The piper's hated voice drifted back to me on the air. *I'll see you at the very center of town at the eighth chime of the grand clock tomorrow evening, he said. Have my coin and the culprit, or everyone you love will die.*

Sometime later, long after the music had faded away, I heard light steps on the carpet behind me and felt a cold, wet nose nudging my leg. At that touch, the lock on my muscles loosened, and I was finally able to take a step. I ran to the door and out onto the sidewalk.

It was late. The night was silent and empty. All along Arcane Avenue, lights were off and storefronts were closed.

High above me, the night sky was black velvet peppered with silver pinpoints of light that seemed to pulse through the darkness. The moon was full, its shadowed silver surface seeming to mock me as I stood alone and bereft on the sidewalk.

Behind me, Vel softly whined.

I turned to find her staring at me with a soft black gaze. I dropped to my knees in front of her, pulling her close. "Why didn't it snap you up too?" I asked into her soft fur.

Another whine and a tentative wag of her tail was the only response she could give me.

I dropped to my butt and leaned against the warm brick of Croakies' storefront. Vel settled against my hip, sighing deeply and lowering her head to sleep. "The sprite's going to love you," I said, without thinking.

Sebille!

I hadn't seen Sebille get pulled into the piper's coercion. Maybe he hadn't gotten her! I reached into my pocket and tugged out my cell, dialing her number with fumbling fingers. It rang and rang but she never answered. I finally disconnected, knowing with everything inside me that she'd been grabbed too.

I stared at the starlit sky, my heart leaking out of my body in a constant flow of tears, and tried to wrap my mind around a plan.

I needed to somehow figure out a way to save everybody. The solution probably had to start with getting those gold coins. Then I had to convince King Rhorr to offer himself up as a sacrificial lamb to the piper.

Then I needed to somehow capture the piper and get his pipe.

And I had less than a day to do it all.

17

THEY ARE DRAWN TO THE KIND OF
HEART AND THE KEEN OF MIND

I was pounding on the door to Enchanted Collateral at six o'clock the next morning. The shop didn't open until nine o'clock, but I knew that the owner, a giant by the name of Theopolis Gargantu, Theo for short, was an early riser. Like most giants, Theo loved "stuff." He liked to collect it, store it, cherish it, and hold onto it as long as he was physically able.

That made him a great resource, but working with him was a challenge since even if he had what I needed in the shop, it was like pulling molars from a dragon to get him to part with it.

As I expected, Theo was awake. A moment after I knocked, the lights came on inside the shop and Theo's big form appeared in the window.

His face lit up when he saw me. He quickly unlocked the door, yanking it open. "Naida keeper!

What a wonderful surprise." He wrapped dinner-plate-sized hands around my arms and yanked me into a hug that smelled like sugar cookies. I would normally have struggled out of the embrace as quickly as possible, not being a particularly huggy person. But, under the circumstances, it felt really good. So good, in fact, that it brought tears to my eyes. "I'm glad you're okay," I told him.

He pulled back, setting me gently away from him so he could observe my leaky face. "Naida, keeper, what's wrong?"

His gaze slid down to the small green creature near my feet, and he frowned.

"I have a problem. A really big problem. I need your help."

He patted me awkwardly on the head, the action nearly shoving my skull into my shoulders like a turtle. I tried not to grimace but lost the battle. I was too raw to effectively hide my emotions.

"Come. I'll make tea."

Remembering the bag in my hand, I forced my lips to curve into a smile. "I brought donuts."

Theo inclined his chin, his mood sober to match mine. "A donut will be much appreciated." He motioned toward the door at the back of the store. "Come."

"Oh. Um..." I felt all the color leave my face. I wasn't up for his artifact. I wasn't sure I had the energy or intelligence at that moment to navigate it.

A giant's residence was a living, breathing entity. An artifact. As such, it had a life of its own and you never knew what to expect when you walked into one.

Like their owner, a giant's home artifact was generally kindly and benevolent. But the rooms tended to crave clutter and accumulations of stuff. And that clutter always seemed to be moving around. Sometimes very aggressively. They didn't know their own strength and thought nothing of plowing a hapless visitor to the ground in an attempt to greet them.

Theo's seven-foot-tall, five hundred pound body turned to me, realizing with his usual intuition that I wasn't up to navigating his living quarters.

"Ah." He gave me a sweet smile. "No worries." He gave a shrill whistle and the door to his artifact swung open, a silver tray filled with a teapot and three cups clinging to its surface as it rode the space between us like a river rapid. It zoomed past Theo, headed straight for me, tea sloshing liberally from cups.

I started to duck, but Theo reached out and snagged it before it could decapitate me with its greeting. "There now. We'll just sit out here then, shall we?"

I gave him a grateful smile. Climbing onto a stool at the long glass counter, I examined the thousands of items inside the display case while he fussed with the tea things.

"Cream?" he asked. "Sugar?"

I nodded yes to both and he handed me a steaming cup.

He looked down at Vel. "Tea?"

The demon dog barked happily, wagging her tail. He settled a pretty china cup on the floor and extracted a donut from the bag, breaking it into pieces and placing it on a saucer before setting it on the floor next to the cup. "Mind your manners now. That china belonged to my grans."

Vel barked again and took a few dainty licks of the tea before gobbling up a bite of donut.

Theo observed the little creature with a guarded look.

"I hope you don't mind my bringing her," I said.

"Not at all. I had one that looked a lot like her when I was a child." He lifted his dark, deep-set gaze to me, a question in the arched eyebrows. "Where did you get her?"

"New Baal."

The brows arched higher. "You visited the demonic plane?"

I nibbled my donut. "We did."

"You must tell me all about it."

I nodded. "I will. I promise. But right now, I need your help."

"Of course. What can I do for the Office of the KoA?"

I frowned. The way he'd stated the question told me he was stepping out of the friend space and offering me his professional services. I tried not to be offended by it. When dealing with the objects of his livelihood, Theo was all business. I quickly filled him in on the highlights of the past few days.

His expression went from polite interest to intrigue and then to horror as the story unfolded. When I told him what the piper was demanding, he looked grim. "I'm guessing you came to me hoping I'd have the thousand guilders?"

I thought about how best to make my request. Theo usually needed finessing to get him to let go of a treasure. But I didn't have the energy for complex negotiations. So I just asked. "I only need one. Do you have a single guilder I can buy?"

I didn't have any idea what a guilder would cost in the current market. Gold prices changed value on a daily, even hourly scale. Adding to the complexity, guilders weren't common. The chances Theo would have one seemed slim. But I had no idea who else to ask.

He pursed his lips for a beat, then dunked a chocolate cake donut in his tea and took a large bite. Chewing slowly, he stared at me in a way that made me feel like he was accusing me of something.

I stared back. I was desperate and had no place

else to go. "If you don't have any guilders, maybe you know of a friend who can get me one?"

"When do you need it?" Theo asked, licking his fingers.

"Today. As soon as possible." If I managed to get one, I'd need a few hours with the coin to do what I needed to do with it.

His eyes went wide. "Today? Oh my. That's a tall order, Naida keeper."

I simply stared at him. It was what it was.

"Do you have any guilders, Theo?" My voice broke on the question because I could tell by his reaction that he didn't. Tears burned my lids. I blinked rapidly to expel them. Down by my feet, Vel whined softly and licked my ankle with her rough tongue.

Theo stared at the little dog. I really wished I could read the expression on his wide face.

He leaned back against the counter, and it groaned. I flinched, hoping it would hold. "What do you know about these creatures, Naida keeper?" He nodded toward Vel to indicate he meant the demon dog.

"Not much. She's really sweet. And she can roar like a dragon when she wants to." I grinned at the memory of how she'd scared the demons on the crumbling walkway into turning on their heels and running back the way they'd come.

He nodded. "They have many talents. That is

one. I was actually referring, though, to their behaviors and personalities. They are notoriously particular about who they spend company with." His gaze lifted to mine. "They are drawn to those who are kind of heart and keen of mind. They have little patience for evil and have been known to eradicate villains with great skill."

I looked down at Vel and she cocked her head, her soft black eyes brimming with affection. "I had no idea."

He crossed his arms over his wide chest, nodding. "She is with you because you need her."

I thought about telling him she was with me because her previous owner was a jerk, and Hobs stole her away from him, but I didn't bother. It didn't really matter anyway.

In fact, I wondered why he'd gotten diverted by it. "Theo..."

He held up a hand to stop me. "I tell you this because it explains why I do what I am about to do." He held up a finger. "Drink your tea. Eat your donut. You will need energy for what you have ahead of you, Naida keeper. I will be back."

Excitement tightened my chest. Was it possible he had the coin? Could I really be that lucky? I finished my tea and donut, reaching for another donut as I heard the thumping and crashing I expected from the roiling beehive of Theo's artifact. At any given moment, he was probably in danger of being clocked by a flying golf club or smothered by a friendly pillow.

I broke the donut in half and gave Vel one piece. I bit into the other half. By the time I finished my donut, Theo was stumbling out of his living quarters, his shirt askew on his shoulders and a very large feather sticking out of one ear.

He swung at the feather and tugged on his shirt, grumbling to himself.

I fought a grin. "Trouble with the artifact?"

He shook his buffalo-sized head. "It has been unruly lately." He skimmed me a quick, secretive look. "Change makes it antsy."

I lifted my brows. "Change?"

He flapped a hand in dismissal. "It's nothing. I'll just give it a good spring cleaning and put it all to rights."

He held his big hand out to me, fingers folded around something. When he opened his hand, a single gold coin lay in his palm. "My gift to you."

I blinked in surprise. "No, Theo, I..."

He took my hand and placed the coin into it. "The people you want to help are my friends too. I wish to do my part."

"That's..." I gave up trying to keep tears from falling. "Thank you."

He nodded solemnly. "Please don't tell anyone, though. They'll be breaking down my door trying to get my stuff."

I laughed wetly. "Promise."

"It was the demon dog," he told me.

"What?"

"She trusts you. It is a testament to your innate goodness. I cherish that quality above all things."

I gave him an impulsive hug, inhaling his sugar cookie scent for a long moment before letting go. "Thank you. I'll get this back to you if I can. I promise."

He waved a dismissive hand, but I saw the gleam in his eyes. He'd take it if I could bring it back. He was a giant, and giants gathered stuff. They rarely gave it away. Which made his gift to me all the more precious.

"If I can help with anything else. Let me know."

I opened the door. Vel trotted through before me. "I'd love some backup tonight if you feel like it," I told him.

A wide grin split his face. "I'll bring Birte."

My grin matched his. "Perfect." I could do worse than having a giant and a silver dragon at my back.

Much, much worse.

Closing the door behind me, I looked down at Vel, buoyed by her happy little face. "Okay, girl. Now for the hard part. We need to go talk to the king."

18

HE LOOKED LIKE A KING WHO WAS
GOING TO WAR

I was understandably nervous about my visit to the ogre kingdom outside of town. The last time we'd been there, things had been a wee bit tense. But at least I'd had backup then.

The thought made me pull out my cell and try Sebille's number again. She hadn't answered the last dozen times I'd tried. But hope springs eternal, as they say.

Hope crashed around my sneakers when the phone continued to ring, unanswered. I finally disconnected, blinking back tears.

As I strode onto the hard, rocky land with Vel at my side, I couldn't miss the hostile looks being thrown our way from the unusually large presence of ogres along the boundaries.

I hadn't gone more than ten yards before several especially big ones stepped from the shadows around the rocks. Unlike the brightly hued forms of many of the ogres we'd met, the watchers' bulky bodies were the same color as the stone they'd melted into. I wondered if their size and chameleon-esq melding abilities denoted them as a different type of ogre. I made a mental note to ask Maxine. If she was still talking to me after the Pied Piper mess was over.

I told them I needed to speak to the king.

Vel and I were escorted all the way to the portal that fed King Rhorr's throne room. Our escorts stopped at the gateway, their bulky bodies straight and stiff, gazes locked on the portal.

A moment later, the gel-like substance inside the portal rolled and rippled and the king stepped out.

He wore a forest-green robe that danced around his thick ankles when he moved. There was no white edging the robe. In fact, there were no flourishes at all. The wide belt at his waist held the largest sword I'd ever seen. His usually wild white hair and beard had been woven into small, tight braids. A green band, studded with gems as large as my thumbnails, surrounded his head.

He looked like a king who was going to war.

Rhorr's blue eyes still held the fire of anger, and the worry that formed the real basis of his thoughts was hidden behind that fire. His bulky features were set in stone as hard as that which surrounded us. "Do you have the culprit?" he demanded.

I barely kept from wincing. "That's what I came to speak to you about. Can we talk in private?"

He flung his head back and roared, the sound making me jump. "The time for talk is over. You must turn him over to me now."

Dredging up every bit of courage I had, which wasn't a lot under the best of circumstances, I shook my head. "You gave me thirty-six hours. I have eleven hours left."

I felt rather than saw the tension sweeping through our escorts. The atmosphere grew thick with it. So thick that my lungs struggled to pull air.

Vel whined softly, pressing against my leg.

I lowered my voice and inclined my head in a bow. "Please, your majesty?"

Rhorr grunted impatiently, but I assumed that was meant for his guards. "Come."

I touched Vel's soft green head and started forward, not giving him time to change his mind.

If Vel was startled by the strange, gelatin-like quality of the portal magic, she didn't show it. She bounced through ahead of me, tongue lolling and tail working overtime.

I stumbled slightly as the resistance of the portal gave way but found my balance again before I embarrassed myself.

By the time I stepped out of the portal, Rhorr was already pacing in front of his throne, hands clasped at his back and eyes dark with worry.

I watched him for a moment, thinking he was working up to whatever he wanted to say. After several moments, I realized he wasn't going to be the first to speak. "King Rhorr, I have a plan to capture the piper." I hesitated a moment, knowing what I was about to request was likely going to send him into orbit.

Vel leaned against my leg and my fingers found her fur, pulling comfort from her support and warmth.

Rhorr stopped pacing and looked at me, his bushy white brows peaking in question.

"I need your help to capture him," I finally said.

He blinked in surprise. A pleased smile crossed his face. "Of course. I'll gather my army and..."

I held up a hand to stop him. "That's not what I meant." I realized too late I'd interrupted him, and his ego was none too pleased about it.

He puffed up like a balloon, his face turning purple. "How dare you!"

Vel trembled against my leg, but I'd reached intimidation overload. In fact, I was just generally overloaded. I had a healthy dose of stress myself, and I'd had it with being bossed around and intimidated.

I lifted my chin, letting my anger and frustration show in my eyes. The world turned silver around the edges, and I realized my eyes were glowing from the power of my magic.

Rhorr's eyes widened, and his mouth snapped shut.

"I dare because I stand to lose everything. Everyone I care about. He's taken them, King Rhorr. He's taken all my friends and the ones I love. He'll kill them if I don't meet him at the gazebo in Enchanted Park. He's demanding two things. The thousand guilders the Mayor of Hamelin stole from him." I hesitated only a beat so he wouldn't miss my next words. "And you."

Surprise lit Rhorr's face again. "Me?"

I nodded briskly. "He has anointed Enchanted as Hamelin in his fractured mind, and you have become his nemesis, the Mayor."

"But why?"

I threw up my hands. "How in the goddess's farting pet poodle do I know? The man's insane."

Rhorr thought about it for a beat, and then his face turned sad. "Naida, child, I don't have a thousand guilders."

Relief flooded me. He didn't refuse to help. "I think I have that covered. Will you come with me to the gazebo tonight? Will you play prisoner?"

King Rhorr's smile soothed my roiling belly. "Let me get my advisers. We'll figure something out that will meet your needs."

I expelled a relieved breath and did something really impulsive. I stumbled forward and wrapped my arms around him, giving him a hug. My arms barely passed his sides, but he chuckled and patted my back.

"Thank you," I said, tears stinging my eyes.

By the time Vel and I climbed into my little beetle bug car, I'd lost almost three hours of my precious stash of time. I sped toward Croakies, regretting the time my visit had taken but knowing it couldn't be helped. King Rhorr and his advisors had come up with a good plan. A plan that would hopefully keep everybody safe.

But it all hinged on getting hold of that pipe before the piper could use it against us.

Walking into Croakies nearly took me to my knees. The store was dark and silent. The building felt worse than empty.

It felt devoid of life.

In my apartment, I got Vel a bowl of water and grabbed a bottle of water for myself. I'd briefly considered making tea but decided I wasn't up for it. I couldn't think about eating either, but I dug through my fridge, looking for meat scraps to give Vel.

She ate with a ravenousness that made me feel guilty. I added more food to her bowl, scratching her neck before moving away to descend the steps. The communicating mirror was about two-thirds repaired, the sections where the glass had fused back together showing only the finest lines where the breaks had been. I knew that, over time, even those would fade away. Positive magic repaired itself from the positive energy around it.

Until the hated piper had danced his way into our lives, Croakies had been full of positive energy. In my current state, I wasn't sure I even felt that energy in the place anymore.

I shoved that depressing thought away and sent a ribbon of keeper energy into the mirror, bracing myself for the conversation to come.

My magic swirled silver ribbons through the mirror, disappearing where it flowed through the still-missing chunks of glass. I waited as the energy churned across its surface, starting to tense when the magic wasn't answered.

"Come on, Madeline," I said under my breath. "This is no time to ignore my call."

The silver energy twirled and spun, slowing as time passed. Finally, the magic oozed away and the mirror's reflective surface returned.

No answer.

I bit back a swear, lifting my hand to call again. I never made that call. In the next moment, the front door of Croakies slammed open, crashing against the wall behind it.

I took off running, Vel bounding at my feet. Yanking keeper energy to my fingers as I pulled open the door, I sent a ribbon of it skyward, hearing the nearly immediate swish of displaced air as I stepped through the dividing door.

A beat later, Blackbeard's sword was in my hand, and SB was tumbling through the air toward my intruder.

The out-of-control parrot smacked hard into the intruder's face and squawked as the wizard sent a jolt of oily black energy into his tail feathers. "Bwawk! Devil take ye, rat-faced cur! A bilge rat ye are and a bilge rat ye'll be. Blackbeard's sword will double thee. Though this half will crumple and that half will fall, ye'll still be a bilge rat once and for all!"

The wizard stared at the undead bird with a look of disbelief, hands out and energy spinning around them just in case the parrot should decide to attack.

Or just insult him some more in incomprehensible language.

"What are you doing here?" I asked. I swished the blade from side to side, setting my feet for battle. I could see the form of my attack in my mind even as I addressed my unwelcome visitor.

"I want that pipe," the wizard demanded, his dark face hard. I eyed him up and down, seeing a man on the edge of his control, with contempt for the person he viewed as standing in his way.

For those of you who haven't been paying attention, that would be me.

"What makes you think I have it?"

"I saw it come to you." He stepped forward, hand outstretched. "Give it to me, or I'll kill your little friend there."

I shrugged, thinking he meant SB. "Good luck catching him. He's a much better flier than he appears."

Of course, the parrot took that moment to trip over a random wisp of air and go beak over tail feathers across the store to smack into the door we'd just come through. Ragged red and green feathers sifted to the rug as we watched him slide bonelessly toward the ground.

The wizard lifted a brow. "You were saying?"

"He's undead," I told him. "And besides..." The sword sang through the air, my arm magicked into performing a beautiful display of the blade's deadly intentions. When I held the sword, its magic infused me, turning me into a swordswoman with mad skills and grace. As well as making me want to say stupid things like *shiver me timbers*, and *pass the grog*. "The sword protects him."

The wizard's cold, dismissive gaze told me he didn't respect the bird or me. But the blade...

"Naida keeper, hand the pipe over and I'll leave. You'll never see me again."

"I don't have it."

"Don't lie to me!" he roared. His expression turned even darker than before. The telltale dark veining rose along his arms. He was about to go full black acid death on me.

The sword vibrated with latent energy, the sweet ping of it infusing my limbs. I danced lightly on my feet, one arm lifted above my head as I leaped forward, performing a graceful arc that should have taken off his head. Somehow, he sidestepped my attack, a nimble move that had him spinning toward Vel and dropping to one knee, black ooze dripping from his palm and sizzling sulfurous holes into the rug. "I'll kill the pup."

My heart slammed against my ribs. Stars danced before my eyes.

I hesitated, fighting my fear, but the sword only understood one thing. When attacked, fight back. Suddenly I was skipping across the floor, forcing him to backtrack or eat my blade. The sword was a blur, performing a deadly jab, a lethal slice, and a spinning parry as the wizard sent a jet of black energy toward me.

My movements were so fast he couldn't target me with his magic. He fired off a bolt of power that sizzled against the wall behind where I'd been, the magic burning a fist-sized hole in the drywall.

Possum peepers! It was going to cost me a fortune to repair all the damage.

Blackbeard's sword sliced toward George's hands. If we could sever them at the wrists, his foul magic would be stopped. Black blood welled from a deep cut on one wrist, but it wasn't enough to stop him.

Vel sat calmly, watching the show. She didn't seem overly concerned about the wizard, but it was possible she'd never encountered the wizard's despicable type of magic in the demonic plane.

As the sword cut a thin slice along the wizard's side, black goo oozed out of the wound and ran down his leg to the ground.

My carpets burned and buckled under the toxic magic, and I wanted to cry.

The wizard dipped his fingers into the acid and flung it at me.

The oily black ooze hit me on the arm and it burned like fire, yanking an agonized scream from my throat. The sword clattered to the ground, the toxic sludge surging forward as if hungry to devour the powerful artifact. I reached for the weapon, but the poisonous muck found my fingers, and I had to backtrack, cradling my arm against my belly.

Vel barked at the wizard, growling low in warning as he started toward me. His hands dripped with the caustic stuff, and I knew without a single doubt that he intended to wrap himself around me and burn me alive with it.

I threw keeper magic at the sword. It rose off the ground, wobbled on the air, and then fell back to the carpet. The wizard's acidic magic flowed over it, hissing like a nest of poisonous snakes as it covered the magical weapon.

There was a thump across the room. I turned to find SB on the floor, unmoving.

"No!" Tears filled my eyes.

"Give me the pipe!" the wizard screamed in my face. He lifted his hands to either side of my head and pressed his face, nearly covered in the bulging black veins, close to me. "Give it to me, or you'll die, Keeper."

I straightened my spine and looked into his cold, black eyes. "I can't give it to you."

"Can't? Or won't?" he asked, sneering.

"I can't. I don't have it. But even if I could, I wouldn't give it to you. You're evil enough without being able to compel people." I threw out a hand, sending a ribbon of magic toward the artifact library. A heartbeat later, the door flew open, and a coiled rope smacked into my palm. I took several steps back to give myself room and then spun the rope into the air, using the cowboy magic that saturated the arti-fact to send the rope spinning right to its target.

The coil of rope slipped over George's head and tightened around his upper arms.

With a roar of rage, the wizard lifted his forearms and managed to fling a hand toward my face.

I ducked away, but the room around me shifted, slowed, and I found myself staring into the wizard's frozen face. Black droplets hung suspended around his curved fingers, moving so slowly I wouldn't have seen them shift unless I'd been looking.

I stepped away from the magic, feeling as if I were trying to walk through waist-deep water. Utter silence filled my ears. I looked around in shock, wondering what had happened.

The bubble broke, and the strange sense of slowed time fell away. George's hands lifted to fling more flesh-eating magic at me, but I was no longer there.

I infused the lariat with a pulse of my magic and yanked it hard. The wizard flew over my head, his skull crashing into the nearest bookshelf hard enough to make it wobble from the impact. His hated eyes rolled back in his head, and he slid bonelessly to the floor.

Vel yipped.

"Did you do that time-stopping thing?"

She panted, giving me a doggy grin.

The exterior door slammed open again. I spun toward the noise, wanting to scream.

What else could possibly go wrong?

Shock wrenched my eyes wide. "Sebille?"

She looked from me to the wizard. "Will Rogers' lariat?"

I nodded. "I knew it would come in handy someday."

"Icy." Sebille looked at Vel, frowning. "What's that?"

Vel barked happily.

"*That* is the reason the wizard is currently face down in a burning puddle of his own magic excrement," I told her, unable to quash a grin at seeing the sprite.

She shook her head. "You can explain later. Right now..." She hurried over and placed a small metal box next to the wizard, opening the tiny door on the side.

The box sent a fog of magic out to cover the wizard. He shrank quickly, retreating into the box along with his nasty magic.

Sebille closed the door and placed her hand over it. Green sprite energy flared from her palm, and the door disappeared. She stood up, wiping her hands on her purple and green polka-dot dress. "That's done. Now..." She looked at me. "How are we going to get everyone back from that demon-turd piper?"

With a happy squeal, I threw myself at her and hugged her hard enough to make her yelp. "I'm so glad to see you."

"Ugh!" she said. "Get off me." Despite her words, she didn't fight me too hard.

"I can't help it," I said, a stupid grin on my face. "I thought he'd gotten you too." I frowned. "Why haven't you been answering your phone?"

She flushed. "I left it in my room."

Lizard on a landline!

I let go of her and stepped back, narrowing my gaze. "Where have you been?"

"I've been looking for that wizard." Her tone let me know it was a stupid question. "I finally found him a little while ago, and he got away again." She frowned accusingly at the box. "I caught a whiff of his magic signature about a mile from here and took a chance he was coming to Croakies." She eyed Vel again. "Is that a demon dog?"

"It is." I smiled down at the little green pup. "She did something to slow down time so I could stop him. It was the bee's britches!"

Sebille nodded. "Good job, dog."

Vel barked as if she understood. I was starting to think she might.

"So what happened in New Baal?"

I sighed. "Really long story. We might need tea and brownies."

"I'll fix the tea," Sebille said. Her instant agree-ableness told me she needed the tea as much as I did.

"I'll get the brownies out of the hidey-hole."

We had to hide the sweet treats in a special spot behind the cabinets because of Hobs. To a hobgob-lin, brownies were like crack cocaine. Even as I had the thought, sadness tightened my chest. Hobs was gone. Along with Wicked, Slimy, Fenwick, and sweet little Baca. Grym was gone too, and Bandy Joe. And the fae! How was I going to tell Sebille her mother had been taken?

My friends were all in danger because I'd made a selfish deal with King Rhorr.

"It's not your fault," Sebille said in a rare moment of compassion.

I was so shocked I couldn't speak.

She rolled her eyes and handed me tea, sitting down at the table next to me. "I can read you like a book. It's not your fault or mine that we agreed to go after the piper to get out of the contract. We would have gone after him anyway. King Rhorr's offer was just a bonus."

She was right. I knew it deep down. But still... "He took your mom and the fae too," I told her, my voice soft.

She nodded. "I know."

"You know? How? Were you here when he took them?"

She nibbled a brownie, shaking her head. "I went to the greenhouse and they were all gone. Then I went to Lea's. And came here..." Her words trailed off, and I saw the fear in her iridescent green eyes.

"I'm sorry, Sebille. I couldn't stop him."

She tucked a bright strand of hair behind one pointed ear. "Wipe the Gloomy Greta look off your face and help me come up with a plan to catch this guy."

I took a bite of brownie, the chocolate jump-starting my brain. "Oh. I already have a plan."

Sebille looked dubious. "What is it?"

After a bracing sip of tea, I told her about the piper's demand that I show up with King Rhorr and the thousand guilders at eight o'clock in the park. Then I told her about my meeting with the king and about Theo's offer for him and Birte to help.

When I was done, she looked crestfallen. "Where are we going to get that kind of money? Especially that particular coin. I'm sure there aren't a lot of guilders lying around Enchanted."

"Theo had one," I told her.

"One? Great. Now, all we need to do is find nine hundred and ninety-nine more."

"Not necessarily," I murmured, sipping my tea. I determinedly avoided her gaze.

I saw the moment she understood. "No, Naida. It's too dangerous."

"It will be okay," I said, knowing she was right.

But the sprite was shaking her head so hard I was afraid she was going to break something in her neck. "Those people who died from that artifact only used it a handful of times. You're talking about using it a thousand times?" She stood up and grabbed my cup as if she were cutting me off. "I'm not going to let you do it. That thing is highly toxic."

"There *is* another way." She'd been heading back

to the tea area, but she stopped in her tracks, whipping around to glare at me.

I flushed, knowing she was going to hate my alternative idea even more. "We can make the piper do it."

19

LIKE A JESTER IN A BAD MEDIEVAL MOVIE

I shoved my hand into the pocket of my jeans, my fingers fumbling with a small cloth pouch that had a distinctive round object inside. I'd been trying not to fidget, knowing the movement had a good chance of giving us away before we even got started.

But my nerves were getting the best of me.

A constant chorus of soft rustling sounds reminded me that life went on around me. No matter how much drama my life brought me, things beyond my sphere just kept plodding along. It was a sobering thought. Comforting, in its own way. But it did nothing to soothe my nerves.

What we were about to do was complicated and risky. All the parts needed to come together in the right way for it to work. The chances of that happening were low enough to make my stomach twist and roil with nervous queasiness.

And beneath it all was a bone-deep sadness that my friends were in danger. Desperate, unfathomable danger. I had no idea where they were...what state their minds were in...or how I'd save them.

I only knew I had to save them.

That one certainty was locked into my awareness, carved into every thought, and infusing every rise and fall of my chest.

I looked up as a fast-moving bank of clouds skidded past in a dark silver sky, revealing a fat silver moon whose light filtered through special carvings in the gazebo at Enchanted Park. The gazebo was located at the very center of the city of Enchanted, and was a magic-enhancing artifact that fed the moon's energy into the structure through those carvings, tripling any magical energy used beneath its roof.

I was sure the piper intended to use that to his benefit.

Hopefully, we were a few steps ahead of him in that.

Sweat dripped down between my shoulder blades, cooling my skin in the warm breeze. I'd pulled my long, brown hair back in a high ponytail to get it off my neck, but wisps of it had escaped and were clinging to my wet skin. Unfortunately, mosquitoes viewed the exposed flesh as an invitation to an all-you-can-eat Naida buffet.

Movement flashed at the edge of the trees, and I

instinctively shrank back. I prayed it wasn't one of my people breaking ranks.

Vel gave off a low growl, soft enough that I felt its vibration on the air more than heard it. I reached down and scratched between her perky, tufted ears. "Steady," I whispered as a familiar, lean figure stepped into view. I frowned.

How could that be?

The wizard George slid a midnight black gaze around the clearing. He glanced at the slender figure who was suddenly standing in the center of the gazebo, nodding. Where in the name of the goddess's favorite pool boy had *he* come from?

The Pied Piper stared directly at the spot where I stood, "Come out, Keeper. Don't be coy."

"Stay with me," I whispered to Vel, before stepping out of the trees. I moved to a spot several yards away from the wizard and the gazebo and stopped, keeping my distance.

Grinning smugly at me, George gave me a mocking little bow. "Naida keeper. I'd say it was a pleasure, but having my nose hairs pulled by a troll with long fingernails would be a pleasure compared to dealing with you again." He cocked his head. "Still...it's worth it to see the expression on your face."

I silently willed my crew to stick to their assigned roles. The wizard's presence there definitely put a crimp in our plan, but I thought we could still make it work. "Funny," I told him, trying to keep my tone light. "I could have sworn you were drooling into your own slimy magic the last time I saw you."

He laughed. "I can see how you might think that." He lifted his arms, and I tensed for his attack. Instead, there was a flash of graphite-colored smoke, and a less-familiar but equally repulsive face was staring back at me. It was the second wizard we'd banished to the void with George. I'd never learned his name. I hadn't cared enough.

The image wavered and changed back to George and then back to wizard x. "Who am I? Such a conundrum, yes?" He seemed so proud of himself, I decided to let him tell me how clever he'd been. In the meantime, I could sense my people moving closer. "Okay, I give. Tell me how you escaped the prison box?"

His laughter was slightly unhinged. No surprise there. "I didn't actually escape." He made a faux sad face. "I'm afraid that was Lyle. He's always been a little annoying. You wouldn't believe how annoying. Stuck in the void with that loser, I nearly lost my mind."

Nearly?

I frowned. "But I'm pretty sure we only brought *you* out of the void. How did Loser Lyle get out?"

The wizard nearly vibrated with joy. "That's the best part, isn't it? You thought I was doing a spell to locate the pipe." He blew a raspberry. "I already knew the piper had taken it into the demonic realm."

Realization hit me. "The spell with the skull. You were releasing Lyle from the abyss."

The wizard gave me a slow clap. "He was very grateful. And he did deserve a chance to get back at you for sending us there. He didn't even mind when I asked him to pose as me."

"You wanted us to think you were out of the way."

He nodded. "Very good, Keeper. Maybe you're not the complete idiot I thought you were."

Vel's growling, which had been getting more emphatic by the moment, turned into snarls. She really didn't like the wizard. I couldn't blame her. "Steady, girl," I warned.

Her snarl ended on a soft whine of complaint.

"Am I to assume you're directing the piper?" I glanced at the figure in the center of the gazebo. Moonlight danced over him in cute little stars and crescent moon shapes, making the figure appear to be moving. Except that he hadn't moved. The piper stood under the magical silver light show, smiling vapidly in my direction.

"He's not real," I mumbled in shocked surprise.

"Oh, he's real," the wizard said. "He's just not the Pied Piper."

I fought through the confusion. "You're the piper?"

George gave me a small bow. "The action has been his. The direction is mine. He's been a fun little puppet for me for centuries. He's gotten me everything I've ever wanted. Don't ever doubt the power of a good blackmail scheme. Especially when the threat is a total loss of autonomy followed by a gruesome death." He grinned. "But it isn't foolproof. I actually did get stiffed on my thousand gilders in Hamelin. That part was true. And the children..." He clucked his tongue. "It really was a shame about them."

Rage made it hard to breathe. The wizard was every bit the monster the Pied Piper mythology portrayed. And worse. "You're not going to get away with this," I growled out.

He laughed gaily. "But, Naida, I already have."

The earth shook beneath my feet, a rhythmic series of mini-earthquakes as Theo's massive form rose above the trees, moving quickly toward us.

High above our heads, a dragon's roar split the night, fire painting a line across the moon.

I looked at George as the tree line bulged outward and a small army of ogres suddenly ringed the clearing around the gazebo. They held spears and battle axes and lengths of thick chain in their hands. Their faces were hard with unrelenting rage. "You can't win this war, George. Give up the pipe, and you might live through it." That was a lie. Grym was going to have his hands full, keeping Rhorr from ripping the wizard into pieces.

There was a flash of light, and George was in the gazebo. The puppet piper was gone. Black energy boiled around the wizard's hands, and he spun in a circle, flinging the energy out around him as he spun. The magic coated the air between the posts of the gazebo, leaving behind a charcoal wall of shimmering energy.

With a blood-curdling roar, the ogres charged. But they were too late.

Not even a platoon of ogres would be able to break through that protective wall. Especially not with the gazebo's magic-enhancement power.

"So, Naida keeper, where are my coins?" George asked with a smug grin. "And where..." He looked around, feigning confusion. "Is my Mayor of Hamelin stand-in?"

I clutched the small bag in my pocket. "You do realize King Rhorr had nothing to do with cheating you."

"Of course, I understand. I might be crazy, but I'm not stupid." He had a good laugh at that. "I just kill myself."

"I wish you would. It would save me the trouble," I told him on a growl.

He laughed again. "I got my revenge on the Mayor a while back. This is just for me. Ogres are a particularly annoying race, don't you think?"

"No, I don't think. I find them fascinating and kind and loving." I glared at him. "Especially the elder you killed with your compelling magic."

He shrugged. "Weak minds. They were so easily compelled. Believe me, I take no pleasure in that, Naida. It's no fun to vanquish such a pathetic enemy."

"They aren't your enemy, wizard. They were just minding their own business. Why don't I just give you the money, and we call it a day? You can release everyone and go about your business. You're out of the void now. You can grab the world by the entrails."

He grimaced. "Ew. I think you got that saying wrong."

"No." I shook my head. "I got it exactly right."

He didn't laugh at that. Apparently, I'd struck a nerve. George glanced up at the moon. "I see your time is up, Keeper. Produce the king and my money, or all your friends will die. Including the ones you've dragged here tonight."

I flinched before I could stop myself. My heart thudded against my chest, and I momentarily saw stars. But I shoved my shoulders back and lifted my chin, releasing a stream of pent-up breath to calm myself. I forced my feet to move forward. One at a time. Eventually, I ended up inches away from the shimmering wall of energy. I could feel its power from where I stood, biting my skin like red ants. I fought the urge to rub my arms and thrust the little leather pouch toward him.

The wizard frowned. "What's this?"

"It's your money."

His face turned a deep shade of red and his cold black gaze roiled with power. I heard the energy snapping around his fists before I saw it. "You dare to cheat me again!"

With a sigh, I tugged the string and pulled the pouch open, reaching into it with two fingers to pull out two golden coins. "I put one guilder into this, and the artifact duplicated it. If I put these two back..." I demonstrated by doing exactly that, tugging the silk chord tight with the coins inside. A tiny burst of golden light flared through the pores of the fabric, and something ugly slithered up my arms to lodge in the base of my brain.

Greed.

I knew it would only grow with each use, poisoning my brain until I'd do anything for the gold it created. Which was why Sebille hadn't wanted me to use the pouch to create the ransom.

I shoved the sprouting seed of avarice aside as I dug out the four coins and showed them to him. "You can make a thousand coins. Or two thousand. Or a hundred thousand." I licked my suddenly dry lips, thinking how wonderful it would be to have that much money. I wondered what the value of each coin was. It had to be hundreds of dollars. How quickly that would add up...

"...give that to me?"

I blinked, ripped from my thoughts, and forcefully shoved aside a nagging desire to keep the pouch. "What?"

"Why would you give me such an artifact? It's worth far more than the ransom I demanded."

I'd already considered a response to the question, knowing he'd ask it. He'd suspect the pouch was a trick. I'd decided to just be honest. "It was the only way I could come up with that many guilders. They're rare." I prayed he wouldn't ask me the obvious. Why hadn't I just made a thousand coins and kept the artifact? I didn't think a man with his ego would be concerned about the artifact poisoning him. He'd believe he was too smart for that. But, just in case, I thought a good deflection was in order. Especially since it was the truth. "And I don't care about this artifact. But I do care about my friends. I want them back."

He stared at me for a long moment and then held out his hand, wiggling his fingers. The pouch flew from my hand and landed in his. He grinned as he felt its weight, quickly pulling the four coins out and then adding them back.

I watched him double his wealth a few times, gleefully crowing each time it worked as promised.

And then I said. "I've fulfilled my end of the bargain. Now, you need to fulfill yours."

He wagged a finger at me. "Uh, uh, uh. There's still one piece to play on the board."

"Please reconsider," I said, my tone sincerely reluctant. "The king isn't a pawn for you to use and abuse."

"Is he not?" He cocked his head. "Bring him to me or die."

The trees behind me rustled, and King Rhorr stepped out. Rhorr's mass of white hair was captured at his temples by a band of gold, inlaid with gems. His beard was woven with similar gems strung on golden thread. He was clothed in a flowing cream-colored robe with a wide, purple sash at his waist. The robe trailed behind him, the pull of the thick grass exposing a pair of slippers that matched the sash.

Something tugged at my heart as I watched him stride into the clearing without a single hesitation. It was the first time I'd truly understood that he actually *was* royalty. It had been hard to meld the idea that he was king with the jolly prankster who'd met Sebille and me naked on a throne...Who'd written a contract on his naked backside so we'd have to take a trip into our nightmares to read and sign the thing... And who'd happily announced that we were to marry two of his favorite ogres as a result of our failure (understandably) to read the fine print at the tail end (sorry, couldn't resist) of said contract.

But at that moment, King Rhorr was every bit a king.

Sebille, who'd escorted the king out of the trees, walked over and stood next to me in the clearing, her expression mutinous.

I looked at her. "What happened? You're supposed to be protecting Rhorr."

"He wouldn't let me. He's afraid the wizard will kill all his people if we fight back."

Tears burned my eyes. "He's going to sacrifice himself?"

She looked away, but not before I saw unshed tears silvering her eyes.

King Rhorr stopped in front of the gazebo and stared at the wizard. "I give myself willingly to you so that you might spare my people from your foul deeds. I'll have your word that you will do this."

The wizard stared at him for a moment and then nodded. "You have my word." But there was a gleam in his eye that had me stepping forward, fully intending to draw Rhorr back and see him safely into the hands of his waiting guards.

I never got the chance.

George pulled a pipe from somewhere on his person and lifted it to his lips. As I watched in help-less horror, he began to play.

King Rhorr jerked, and then started walking. His

big body seemed to be pulled inexorably forward as if drawn by a rope. He stepped through the shimmering wall and stopped before the wizard, dropping hard to his knees on the wooden floor. Eyes glazed, Rhorr bowed his head, every line of his big body going soft in supplication.

The sight infuriated me and I started forward with a cry, falling over a clump of grass and landing on my face. I shoved to my feet, Vel frantically licking my face. A moment later, I was moving again, but I was no longer under my own steam.

King Rhorr's people entered the clearing. They wore dazed expressions on their wide faces, their small eyes glazed as they formed a single file and fell in behind me. Vel stayed near my feet, pressing close enough to keep constant contact with my leg. I wasn't sure, but I thought that one of her abilities was to mute magic, and as long as I was touching her, I could keep hold of my mind, even as my body betrayed me.

We rounded the gazebo in a mindless shuffle, the wizard doing a happy dance as he played. The ground shook as a fifteen-foot-tall giant joined the party, a thick stream of fire flaring high above his head as Birte, his girlfriend the dragon, was dragged into the parade.

When all of the victims had joined the procession, the wizard waved a hand and touched the king's shoulder. "Come," he said, the pipe continuing to play and dance alongside his head without being touched. "It's time to take a long walk off a tall peak."

Like a jester in a bad medieval movie, the wizard danced a jig as he led us through the Enchanted Park woods toward the mountain in the distance.

Was he really going to try to lead us up the mountain and fling us off? Of course he was.

Unless we stopped him.

20

YOU LOOK ALARMED

I thought I'd have more time.

Believing we were headed for the mountain, which had to be two miles away as the crow flies, I'd taken some time to examine the aspects of what I was experiencing.

I'd managed to resist a few things. A finger lift here, a turned foot that took me slightly off course there. It was about what I'd expected. But, what I hadn't expected was the difficulty I'd have in throwing off the inability to speak.

I needed to speak. If only to say one word.

We slogged on through the densest trees I'd ever experienced. Even in the Enchanted Forest, the trees had rarely been packed so tightly together. It was hard to see where we were going. It was nearly impossible to tell where we were.

But, somehow, the wizard led us through the

dense vegetation without smacking us into it. A small miracle on its own.

It took me a while to notice when the space around us grew less restrictive. The trees were thinning, and the sky above showed in more than just the occasional sliver of moonlight through the dense canopy.

A cool breeze finally found us, its gentle fingers a welcome and soothing touch after the humid heat beneath the trees.

Vel's soft footfalls were an ever-present relief as I fought the wizard's compelling magic. She managed to stay close enough to touch at all times. I knew I had her presence to thank for whatever small resistance I'd managed to that point. It was the reason she was there, instead of locked safely in the store.

Things hadn't quite turned out as I'd hoped. But it was possible the little dog was waiting for specific instructions to do her thing. If that was the case, we were all going to be disappointed. At the moment, I couldn't so much as purse my lips to whistle.

We broke fully out of the tree line, and the world opened up in front of us. In fact, it was so open, there seemed to be nothing immediately ahead of us. In the distance, I could just make out the shadowed peak of Mount Enchanted, its snow-covered tip all but glowing in the moonlight.

My first thought was that the emptiness ahead was just a trick of the eye. Until the wizard stepped aside, and King Rhorr kept moving toward what looked like the edge of a cliff.

A wave of dizziness swept through me. Panic ripped at my belly with urgent fingers.

A cliff! Where had that come from?

I watched in helpless fury as Rhorr headed right for the edge. My fingers twitched uselessly at my sides. A scream of warning beat against the back of my throat, unable to escape.

The king's foot stepped to the edge, and rocks tumbled silently downward, the cliff so high and steep I didn't hear the rocks connect with anything for several long seconds.

The pipe went silent, and we stopped in our tracks. Unfortunately, the magic held. I was still locked under its influence.

The wizard walked up to Rhorr and smiled manically into the king's stony face. "No longer the ruler of all things, are you?" he scoffed. "Unable to do a single thing to save yourself or these other fools, aren't you? It's a bitter pill, isn't it, *Your Majesty*?" George bit off the title as if it were almost too foul to utter, clearly hating on poor King Rhorr.

I wondered if it was Rhorr in particular who'd earned the wizard's animosity or if George was rebelling against anyone who had what he considered too much power.

Shaking off the ill-timed musings, I doubled my efforts to break free of the numbing magic. The pipe was silent in George's fist. Its power wasn't gone. But maybe it was weaker since he wasn't playing it?

I tensed my entire body, starting at my feet and moving upward until even my teeth gritted tightly together. I pictured squeezing the invading energy from my muscles and felt a tiny bit of its dark presence fleeing the hostile environment I'd created.

Good. That was good. But how long would it take me to overcome it entirely?

Too long.

Rhorr was a single flick of the wizard's finger away from death.

I released my muscles and tensed again, pushing, straining, tightening...

My jaw softened. I tested the bounds of my new freedom by cracking my lips. As soon as I discovered that I could move my mouth, I wasted no time. "Vel!"

The little dog jolted, peered up at me with her liquid black gaze, and then her jaws began to open, and open, and open, and...

"WOOF!!"

The sound blasted away from her like a sonic boom, so rich with energy it imploded on itself and hit the atmosphere in an inverted vee of sound, a tinny, faraway noise in the center that grew to a T-Rex-level roar that blew everybody's hair back when it found its widest point.

Rhorr stumbled backward, his big fists unclenching and his mighty head turning to the disoriented wizard at his side. The king gave a mighty roar of his own as he pulled back a beefy arm and let loose a punch that sent the wizard flying backward until he crashed into a tree.

The pipe flew out of his hands, into the under-brush several feet away.

I leaped on it, finding myself elbow-deep in a glossy plant with trios of leaves on each stem. My hands felt along the ground and encountered some-thing hard.

But it wasn't the pipe. Blindly feeling around, I touched something that felt like human skin, stretched over bone.

I jerked my hand back with a yelp, scrabbling to my feet. A figure stepped from the trees. A figure with dark cobalt eyes and a slender form.

The Pied Piper's light-brown hair was as straight as a stick and seemed to have a mind of its own. It hung in unruly strands over his pale forehead and stuck out over largish ears.

As before, he wore a robe similar to those we'd seen in New Baal, with hard black boots on his smallish feet. He gave me a satisfied smirk. "Thank you for returning my pipe to me."

"I..." My mind felt torn in half by the new devel-opment. None of our planning sessions had prepared us to deal with two villains. Especially when one of them seemed to come and go at will.

Goddess on a gondola!

The piper tilted his head. "You look alarmed." He shook his head, the strands of light-brown hair lifting away from his skull with the movement. "That one..." The piper nodded toward the wizard, who was still unconscious and hanging like a large, ugly doll from the biggest ogre guard's beefy fist, "...has been the bane of my existence for centuries. He sold me this pipe." The piper looked down at the magical instrument with a mixture of love and hate. "And then used it to control me." Tears filled his dark gaze, moonlight turning them silver as they shimmied down his cheeks. "He made me kill people. Children." Lips quivering with what looked like genuine remorse, the piper shook his head. "Even when you sent him into the abyss, he still controlled me. But I was working on getting free of his clutches. The void made it harder for him to manipulate me. I could finally see a way to be free." The pain in his gaze shifted, turning hard. "But then you brought him back." Without warning, rage tightened his features. "You sentenced me to an unspeakable future of servitude to that monster. You will pay for that!"

I'm sad to say, I reacted too slowly. It was all just too much. How many times would we need to stop somebody from using that stupid pipe?

The piper lifted the instrument to his lips and started to play. Too late, I lunged at him, only to find myself jerked to a stop mere inches from my target, hand stretched toward the pipe.

Behind me, a burst of activity from the others was just as efficiently sliced off. Within the space of a few deadly notes, we found ourselves formed into another tidy line, heading for the edge of the cliff.

Again.

Holy badger boxers! It was time for somebody to write some new material. The "led to their deaths over the edge of a cliff" plot was getting redundant.

Vel bounced up beside me, tongue lolling, and I rolled my eyes down to her. Something in my gaze must have let her know that I was unhappy because she whined. A beat later, she was gone.

King Rhorr's foot hit the edge of the cliff. He started to wobble forward.

A silent scream pulsed in my throat.

Stars burst in front of my eyes.

And Vel lunged. Her jaws clamped onto the pipe and crunched down, breaking it in half.

The music died. For the space of a single heartbeat, the night grew deathly quiet.

Then chaos ensued as the ogres grabbed the unfortunate piper.

And King Rhorr toppled over the cliff on a husky roar of alarm.

21

IT WAS BAD. REALLY, REALLY BAD

"Ah!" I screamed, running for the edge. I dropped to my knees, peering over the cliff. "King Rhorr?" Horror clogged my throat and made the scream come out sounding choked. I cleared my throat as Sebille hit the dirt next to me. Several large bodies dropped down on either side of us.

Silence met my call. I suddenly couldn't breathe. I couldn't see him. But then, the night was pitch black in the enormous depression. Its sheer size eating up the light. We had only the illumination of a cloud-studded moon to see by, and that didn't reach most of the crater. "Rhorr!" I screamed, in a full-on panic.

Nothing.

"Your Majesty!" Screamed one of the ogre guards. The sound of his deep voice reverberated through the canyon, pinging off the rocky walls and sending up echoes.

But there was no response.

I glanced at the sprite. "You need to fly."

Alarm flashed through her gaze, and she bit her lip. But a beat later, she nodded. She shoved to her feet and disappeared behind me.

I turned to the biggest ogre next to me. It was the one who'd called out to the king. His enormous, rock-like body was giving off waves of heat that added to the tension inside my chest. "Can you see anything?"

He shook his big head, staring helplessly into the big, black hole below us. I quickly realized it would be up to Sebille and me to come up with a plan to save the king.

If he wasn't already dead.

I shoved the thought away, hating that it had sifted through my mind. Standing, I rubbed my dirty hands over my jeans, looking around for anything we could use to get to Rhorr.

The ground shook under a series of concussions I realized were footsteps. Theo strode out of the trees and stopped next to me, staring down from his vantage point fifteen feet up. While his size was impressive, I'd seen him go much larger when the situation called for it. "What's happened?" he asked in his deep, giant-sized voice. "I heard a scream."

He'd been at the back of the line and still in the trees when the king had gone over.

"The ogre king fell over the cliff when we took the artifact from the piper." Tears burned my eyes, but I blinked to dispel them. I didn't have time to fall apart. "We can't see him. It's too dark. And he's not answering our calls." My voice broke on the last few words. Theo covered my shoulder with a huge hand and gave it a gentle squeeze. "I've got this."

He turned his face up to the sky and yelled something in dragonish, the same language Sebille and Sadie had spoken in the void.

Birte!

Theo's girlfriend could find the king. She could retrieve him from wherever he'd landed.

My heart started beating at a normal pace again.

High above us, a roar painted fire across the sky. The ogres went very still, eyes skyward, and I saw several huge fists forming.

"It's okay," I told them. "She's one of us."

My gaze slid skyward too. We all stood watching the stunning creature fly toward us. She was mostly invisible in the dark, only showing up when she lit the sky with fire or when the moonlight found the reflective scales covering her sleek frame.

A tiny winged form shot past me to the edge of the cliff and dove straight down.

Sebille had gotten small. I closed my eyes in a silent prayer of thanks that she'd worked through her problem. And then I turned my hopes toward finding the king.

Sebille buzzed back up, flying to me. "He's on a ledge about thirty feet down. He's unconscious and tangled in a tree. I think I see blood."

I grimaced. "Can you heal him?"

"Of course I can heal him, Naida."

I grinned at her snappish tone. The sprite was back.

"But I think it would be best if we bring him up the way he is. I'm not sure he'd let Birte carry him up otherwise."

She was right. One thing I'd learned about ogres in my recent study of them was that they hated and distrusted flying. And that meant they harbored a special distrust of creatures that made the sky their home.

"Right. Okay." I looked at Theo. "Can Birte lift him up here?"

Theo bellowed to the sky again, his voice seeming extra loud in the dark, quiet night.

The dragon's answer was to dive into the canyon and fire up the area around the ledge.

The ogres gasped at the sight, surging toward the brink as if thinking about trying to get to her.

I held up my hands. "She's just trying to see where he is. It's okay."

But the ogres didn't trust the dragon. And, if I'm being honest, they didn't trust me either. They started in my direction, faces hard and body language aggressive. "She'll kill our king," one of them accused.

"She won't," I argued, backing up.

"Well then, why don't we just fling *you* out there and see if the dragon catches you?" suggested a warty, dark green ogre with what looked like unnecessarily large teeth. "Then we'll know if she can be trusted."

Before I could react, hands grabbed me from behind and flung me over a rock-hard shoulder. The ogre lumbered toward the cliff's edge, with me screaming and pounding on his back.

I was like a fly trying to beat up a rhinoceros.

"Let me down, you big idiot!" I screamed.

"Okay," he said, much too happily. He grabbed me around the waist and extended me over the black, gaping maw of the canyon.

Chaos erupted behind us, bodies flying in all directions. The ogre wobbled on the edge, nearly dropping me as panic set in. A second later, an enormous hand snaked out and grabbed the ogre around the back of the neck, yanking him back and away from the edge.

Theo placed him gently on the ground and gave him a little shake. "Let her go. Naida's a friend."

Another roar from below directed everyone's attention back toward the crater. Light pulsed once, then twice, and an enormous form shot skyward, wings quickly beating the air. Birte flew past the moon, and we could see the big, limp form hanging from her claws.

"Bring him back, Birte," I murmured in silent prayer. "Come on. Bring him this way." I had no idea how feral Birte was when in her dragon form. I knew she preferred her native language, which led me to believe she was different mentally in that form.

Theo moved up behind me, his steps heavy and slow. "She'll bring him," he promised.

But she just kept flying, and doubt started to edge in to create panic again.

The ogres were clustered together several feet away. They were clearly unhappy, and I was starting to fear another attack.

Sebille buzzed over and popped into full size. "She's afraid to land here because of the ogres," she reported.

Ah, thank the goddess Sebille understood some dragonish.

Theo nodded. He moved to the brink and, cupping his hands around his mouth, yelled something to the sky.

I glanced at Sebille. She looked worried. "He wants her to drop Rhorr to him."

"Great gargling gorgons," I moaned out. "We'll all be killed."

She nodded, clearly sharing my fear that Theo

would miss or drop the king and the other ogres would kill us all.

We watched in tense silence as the dragon approached, thankfully keeping her fire to herself as she flew. When she was twenty yards out, Theo backed away from the edge and held out his arms. She didn't slow and didn't fly low enough to be grabbed. Theo backed quickly, no easy task with his giantnormous frame. He stumbled once, nearly going down.

Of course, that was the moment Birte decided to drop the king.

"Ah!" The ogres sang out in a horrified chorus. They started forward, realizing their king was plunging toward certain death.

But Theo somehow regained his balance and, knees bent and arms out, caught the limp body before falling backward and skidding several feet along the ground.

The ogres ran forward, grabbing their king in surprisingly gentle hands and laying him across the grass. They huddled protectively over him.

Sebille buzzed over, and a chorus of growls filled the air at her intrusion.

She halted in mid-air, hands on hips. I could almost hear the sprite's eyes rolling. "Stop being idiots," she told the ogres. "Let me heal him."

After another tense moment, the biggest ogre

inclined his head and motioned for the rest to step away.

Sebille stayed in sprite form as she sent pale green healing magic into the ogre king. She buzzed slowly over him, assessing and then repairing whatever she found. A few worrisome minutes later, King Rhorr's eyes fluttered open, and he bolted upright into a seated position. "Where am I? What's happening?"

I relaxed for the first time in what felt like days.

Then I remembered the rest of our missing friends. I looked at Sebille. "Where's the wizard?"

She flew over and popped back to full size, her expression grim. "He's a splat at the bottom of that canyon."

Oh no! "How are we going to find everybody?" I asked.

She frowned. "I don't..."

"The piper!" I said. I turned to the ogres. "Where's the Pied Piper?" I asked.

Blank, unfriendly expressions met mine.

King Rhorr was on his feet. He fixed me with a regal stare. "You found the man who killed Mama Theresa?"

I opened my mouth. Closed it. I wasn't sure. According to the piper, he'd been forced to hurt people. But then he'd tried to kill us, so... "I'm not sure."

Rhorr's bushy white brows lowered. "You're not sure?"

"It's a long story, and I'll be happy to tell it to you. But right now, I need to find out where our friends are. The wizard is dead. The piper might know where they were taken. Will you help me find them? Then we'll work out the rest?"

After a moment's hesitation, he nodded to his men. Two of them disappeared and returned a moment later, dragging the piper between them. He'd been trussed up with thick, scratchy rope around the wrists and ankles. Both eyes were swollen shut, and he was bruised and bleeding over his entire head.

I swallowed hard. For the first time ever, I think I got a full realization of how bad an idea it was to make the ogres unhappy.

It was bad. Really, really bad.

22

A GODDESS-BLASTED OGRE SUMMIT

An ogre summit.

A goddess-blasted ogre summit.

Just when I'd finally realized I wanted to stay as far away from the ogres as humanly possible, I found myself sitting in the middle of a crowd of several thousand of the creatures. Yeah, you heard right. Thousands. Apparently, a decision as large as what to do with the killer of one of their beloved elders required a summit.

I'd begged. I'd pleaded. I'd sicced Sebille and her formidable powers of glaring and eye-rolling on them. But in the end, the king wanted a summit. And a summit we would have.

I'd been a nervous wreck for the two days it had taken for all the ogres within a five-hundred-mile radius to travel to Enchanted. I'd barely slept or eaten. Hadn't been able to perform my duties as a

KoA. I'd tried again to reach Madeline Quilleran but hadn't been successful. As the PTB for the earthly plane, she might have had some influence on King Rhorr. But, it appeared she was MIA.

I had no idea what had happened to my friends. They could be starving, hurt, freezing to death, terrified into madness. It was the worst kind of cruelty to make them sit in limbo while King Rhorr and his advisors argued and planned.

It turned out the ogres considered summits great opportunities to visit and party.

The whole thing made me absolutely irate. It had given me a rash. Or, maybe that was from the shiny, three-leaved plant I'd gotten way too intimate with in the park. Either way, it only added to my torture.

We were forced to sit in the front row of a carefully crafted podium with a large stage where King Rhorr and a dozen advisors sat in throne-like chairs, the piper standing behind them with an ogre on either side and his wrists and ankles chained.

The king had just gaveled the meeting to order. He turned his bright blue, bead-like gaze to me. "As a complainant, Naida keeper, what is your request of this advisory body?"

I gave up scratching my arms, and stood up. Sebille stood too. My Uncle Archie, who'd advised me on how to phrase my appeal to the ogres, stood up on my other side. "Your Majesty, the office of the

Keeper of the Artifacts entreats you to determine the whereabouts of this criminal's victims before you pronounce sentence on him."

The king frowned. "What is the basis for this unusual request, Keeper? The summit has a long list of activities to perform over the next fourteen days. What reasoning do you have for elevating your request to the front of these equally important tasks?"

I bit back a snide reply, knowing it wouldn't help my case. "Your Majesty, with all due respect, your list of tasks isn't time-sensitive. The victims this man was complicit in compelling may be in great danger. It is our opinion that their fate must be placed above those other items."

I chewed my lip as the king glanced at the small, wizened ogre seated next to his throne. "Majit?"

Turning his surly gaze my way, Majit shook his head. His voice was wobbly and rough as he tried to lift it to be heard throughout the summit. "My vote is no, Majesty. This human's concerns do not measure in importance to our people's concerns."

"I agree," said a female with a mountain of snowy white hair and a permanent downward curl to her wide mouth.

A younger ogre, which wasn't saying much in the crowd of obvious elders on stage, raised a bulky arm and gave his bald head a casual scratch. He threw me a smile. "It is my understanding that this human saved our king."

Murmurs slid through the crowd, and thousands of speculative gazes turned my way.

"Further, it is my understanding that she is affianced to one of our people."

Sebille tensed beside me.

A burst of noise down the row from us drew my eye to Maxine, who'd stood up and was grinning around the crowd. Her purple gaze found mine and twinkled as she gave me a coy wave. She shoved at the golden mass of hair on her enormous head, preening for the assemblage.

Laughter rippled through the crowd.

The unnamed bald ogre on the stage winked at Maxine, and she giggled shyly.

The king motioned for Maxine to take her seat and then went down the line of chairs on the stage, requesting votes from the rest of the advisors. An hour later, we had a tie.

King Rhorr would be the tie-breaker.

I all but held my breath as he turned his bright gaze on me. He tapped a finger against his bulbous nose, looking thoughtful.

Sebille was so tense I was afraid she'd crack if someone poked her too hard.

I sent a pleading look toward Rhorr and, a moment later was answered by a twinkle in his bright gaze. "We will resolve the issue of the human victims first."

A roar went up in the crowd, a mix of boos and cheering.

Sweat rolled down my temple. Archie reached for my hand and gave it a squeeze. "Hang tough, child."

Rhorr turned to the Pied Piper. "As the accused in this matter, what say you?"

The piper lifted hate-filled eyes to me and sniffed haughtily. "You can torture or kill me. I will not tell you where they are."

I barely stopped the sob that wanted to escape my lips. I sagged in my chair, tears falling freely down my cheeks. Wicked, Grym, Hobs... I gave a shuddering cry and covered my face.

Sebille made a suspicious sound and began to shake. I turned to find her eyes red and wet with tears. I grabbed her hand and squeezed. She squeezed back.

Archie stood up. "Your majesty?"

Rhorr turned to Archie with a look of surprise. "Void Sorcerer Archibald Pudsnecker?"

Archie bowed low. When he straightened, he started walking toward the stage. "If I might have a word with the prisoner?"

King Rhorr stared at Archie for a long moment.

Archie stood calmly, hands crossed in front of him and expression serene.

Sebille and I exchanged a look. She shrugged.

What was Uncle Archie up to?

Finally, King Rhorr inclined his head. "Very well. You may speak to the prisoner. Would you like to be taken someplace private?"

"No, Your Majesty. That won't be necessary."

Archie moved quickly toward the stage and climbed the steps. He gave a deep bow to the advisers and then walked over to the piper. Leaning close, he whispered something into the man's ear.

I watched in shock as the piper's expression went from belligerent to terrified in the blink of an eye. Archie continued to speak for several more seconds, and then he stepped back. He gave the man what could only be interpreted as a threatening look and then turned away and returned to his seat.

I looked a question at him, but he simply shook his head.

The piper's chains rattled, drawing my attention back to him. He was quivering with fear. The piper tore his horrified gaze from Archie and looked at me. Then he opened his mouth and rocked my world. "I will tell you where they are." He blinked, the horror never leaving his gaze. "I will tell you everything I know."

The rooftop was just the way I remembered it. Though, getting to it was a lot harder than it had been when we'd come there with the wizard. He'd spelled the entire building against entering or leaving.

It had taken Sebille several spells to remove the layers. But, finally, we were standing in front of the metal door leading to George's magical lair. My nerves were a mess. I was almost afraid to know what kind of shape they were in.

I clasped the handle and looked at my two companions. "Ready?"

Sebille frowned. Archie fought to keep his expression neutral. And Vel grinned at me, tongue lolling. Leave it to the dog to put a positive spin on even the most worrisome situation.

I pulled air into my lungs and yanked on the door.

It wouldn't open.

Sebille lifted her hands and bathed the door in pale green light. Still, the magic resisted, screeching as Sebille flung a larger bolt of energy into it. It finally let go on a choking puff of sulfurous black smoke. I stumbled back with the handle in my grip, coughing violently. The sulfurous cloud doubling me over.

Sebille and Archie suffered similar fates, all

three of us leaning against the stair railing as our bodies fought to expel the toxic magic.

"Naida!" a familiar voice called as I finally straightened. Excitement filled me as I looked up to find Lea, holding Hex in her arms and smiling widely. "I knew you guys would come."

I quickly scanned the space, seeing Grym and Mr. Wicked, and Hobs, and Baca, and Rustin and Sadie. Fenwald climbed lazily to his feet and stretched, yawning. The fae burst into enthusiastic flight, flitting excitedly around the space that contained them. They all looked a little worse for wear. All were filthy and too thin. But nobody seemed to have suffered anything too debilitating.

Thank the goddess. I closed my eyes on a silent prayer to the benevolent universe.

We stepped onto the roof, and I realized for the first time that they were all inside an energy prison. The shimmery walls of energy rose from the massive pentagram George had used to release his wizard buddy from the void.

I recognized the same shimmery wall he'd used on the gazebo in the park.

"Are you all okay?" I asked, crouching down to look into Mr. Wicked's sweet orange gaze.

"Meow!" he told me, clearly anxious to escape his prison.

Lea nodded. "We had rainwater. And fortunately,

we had the dinner Joe and Grym picked up before this all happened. It got us through."

Sebille walked along the shimmering wall of energy enclosing them, her palm an inch away from its surface. Lea walked along with her, giving her suggestions for how to remove the barrier. I was sure my friend the witch had been examining the enclosing magic since they'd been locked in there nearly fifty hours earlier.

Sebille nodded, listening intently for a few minutes while I all but vibrated with the need to hug my friends.

Bandy Joe waved, and Zoom peered at me through from his shoulder.

Grym came over and smiled at me through the wall. "Hey." He was holding the green squish in his palm.

I smiled back, tears burning my eyes. "Hey. You okay?"

Grym shrugged. "I'd kill for a really big glass of water."

"We'll have you out of there in a minute."

He nodded. "How's the demon dog doing?"

"She's good."

Vel whined and shifted closer, her tail wagging. She reached her nose tentatively toward the shimmering energy and yelped as it gave off sparks, jumping back.

I looked at Slimy. *Hey, buddy. How's it going?*

He seemed to gather himself, and then Grym winced. "Ew! What did I tell you about peeing on me, frog?"

I couldn't help it. I burst out laughing.

Beside me, Vel's tiny maw started expanding.

"Uh," Rustin said. "What's happening there?"

We all turned to look at the little dog. Everyone took several steps back.

"Gird your loins," I yelled, with a smile in my voice.

"WOOF!!!"

The magic boomed toward the sky, the force smacking my eardrums and blowing my hair off my face. It crashed down around us and slammed into the rooftop hard enough to rock the entire building.

Far below us, windows shattered. Doors slammed open, and voices emerged from apartments that had no doubt been spelled closed since the wizard cast his spell to lock my friends in.

The wall of prison magic enclosing my friends shimmied, bulged outward in a series of giant bubbles, and then popped with a wet hiss of black smoke.

For the second time since stepping onto the roof, we were doubled over coughing again.

Vel happily trotted to Grym and found herself being scooped up for some serious hugs.

Slimy hopped over and looked up at me as I choked.

I'm hungry, sayeth the frog. *There were no flies in there.*

"Miss!" Hobs flew at me. He hit me in the chest just as I straightened and wrapped himself around me as I stumbled back under the force of his greeting. "Hey, buddy!" I cough-laughed, squeezing him tight. "I was so worried about you."

He patted my back. "We were okay, Miss. I promise."

I sniffled, nodding.

Hobs let go and launched himself at Sebille, subjecting her to the same treatment he'd given me. The fae were buzzing around the sprite, and Sebille was smiling at her mom, her eyes suspiciously shiny. At the rate she was going, she was in danger of growing some compassion.

Nah. That was crazy talk.

A warm weight found my ankles and vibrated a figure eight around them. I looked down and saw my cat. I scooped him up, burying my face in his sweet-smelling fur. I couldn't even talk. Tears flooded my face and clogged my throat. He let me hold him for a long moment, purring hard enough to jump-start my heart if it had needed it. Then he nipped me gently on the nose, and I let him go. Fenwald pressed his big, warm body against my legs. I reached down and scratched his ears. "Hey, Fenny."

Rustin touched my arm, gave me a smile, and then went to talk to Archie while Sadie playfully buzzed Vel. The little dog danced around the flitting dragon, happy to make a new friend.

"Come on, everybody," Archie said from the door. "Let's get you home. We'll call for food delivery along the way."

He didn't have to ask twice. Everyone except the fae flooded toward the door. Queen Sindra and her fairies flew into the night, calling out goodbyes as they left.

I grabbed Archie's hand. "Hey, now that I can breathe again, tell me what you said to that piper."

Archie's eyes twinkled. He gave me a slow grin. "I simply told him if he didn't tell us what we needed to know, I'd see that he spent the rest of his life in a void...with Loser Lyle."

I felt my grin growing to match his. "Genius."

He laughed softly and left.

Someone grabbed my arm as I started after him. I turned to find Grym looking at me with more than relief in his dark caramel eyes. "Hang back a minute," he said in a husky voice. "I want to talk to you."

A moment later, the door closed with a loud snick, and Grym ran a hand through his sun-streaked mahogany hair. "I..." he frowned, seemingly unsure how to say what was on his mind.

I waited patiently, happy just to feast my eyes on his broad shoulders and gorgeous face again.

He took my hands in his, clasping them gently between us. "This whole engagement thing..."

I shook my head. "It's off. The king gave Sebille and I a Pre-Annulment Proclamation."

He narrowed his eyes. "Pre-Annulment?"

I grimaced. "Absolving the marriage before it's even a marriage?" I shrugged. "I was unclear. After he said we were absolved of our obligations to Maxine and Rick, I stopped listening."

He nodded, his thumbs making warm circles on my hands. "I didn't doubt you'd find a way out of it." He lifted his gaze to mine. "Maxine's okay?"

My heart melted a little. His kindness always caught me a little bit by surprise. I had no idea why. Probably because he was such a big, strong guy. A cop. I never expected his type to have a gooey center. "She's ecstatic. Apparently, one of the advisors from the summit took an interest in her. I guess he's kind of a big deal." I shrugged.

"Summit?"

I groaned. "I have so much to tell you. But you probably want to get home?"

"I do," he said, his gaze nearly burning a layer of skin off my face. "But first..." Without warning, his lips were on mine. Heat sizzled between us. My belly warmed, and my body melted toward his. I wrapped my arms around him, holding him into the kiss as if I was afraid he'd try to pull away.

But he didn't try to break the kiss. Not even close. In fact, we didn't pull away from each other until the sprite pounded on the door, yelling at us to get a room.

I rested my forehead against Grym's. We were both a little breathless. His big, warm hands were cupping my face, and he seemed reluctant to let go. "I know I made light of the engagement thing," he said. "I'm sorry for that. It was hard on you and the sprite. But I had to make light." He sighed. "Because, if I didn't, I might have done something crazy like challenge Maxine to a duel. The whole thing was making me nuts."

My already gooey middle turned molten with pleasure. "Do ogres even duel?" I asked, a grin in my voice.

He dropped an arm around my shoulders and tugged me close, leading me to the door. "I have no idea. But I knew I couldn't beat her in hand-to-hand combat." He pulled the door open and ushered me through in front of him. "That woman outweighs me by about four hundred pounds. She'd totally kick my...um...fine print."

I dissolved into laughter. "I love a man who knows his limitations."

He tugged me to a stop on the landing, intensity sizzling in his caramel eyes. "And I love a woman..." he kissed my nose. "Whose name is Naida."

My heart stuttered in my chest. Sappy? Yes. But Holy gargoyle kiss Batman! He loved me!

That was it. I was a puddle of goo.

"Give it a rest!" Lea yelled up the steps.

"Jeez, you two!" Sebille objected.

Meow! said the cats in unison.

Ribbit! said the frogs

"Really, Naida. Do you think it's a good idea to hold everyone up like this?" asked Archie.

"Um, hey," Bandy Joe said. "Guys. The dog's doing that thing again."

"Ah!" they all screamed in unison, followed quickly by several pairs of footfalls pounding down the stairs.

Grym and I looked at each other, and our eyes went round. We turned toward the door above and started to run.

Unfortunately, we didn't make it very far.

"WOOF!!!!!"

"Ahhhhhh!"

The End

DON'T MISS OUT

Stay up on all Sam's news by joining her newsletter, and get a copy of a fun mystery just for signing up!

SIGN UP FOR SAM'S NEWSLETTER!

https://samcheever.com/newsletter/

ABOUT THE AUTHOR

USA Today and Wall Street Journal Bestselling Author Sam Cheever writes mystery and suspense, creating stories that draw you in and keep you eagerly turning pages. Known for writing great characters, snappy dialogue, and unique and exhilarating stories, Sam is the award-winning author of 100+ books.

To learn more about Sam and her work, visit her at one
of her online hotspots:
www.samcheever.com
samcheever@samcheever.com